THE HAIRCUT WHO WOULD BE KING

A POLITICAL FABLE

ROBERT TREBOR

PALINDROME PRESS

Copyright © 2019 by Robert Trebor

Published by Palindrome Press

Los Angeles, CA

All rights reserved. No part of this book may be reproduced in any form or by any electronic or mechanical means, including information storage and retrieval systems, without written permission from the author, except for the use of brief quotations in a book review.

Particular emphasis is placed on performance or audio taping of this work *in toto* or in part which is strictly prohibited. For further information, contact the author at **thehaircutgrates@gmail.com**.

This is a work of fiction. Names, characters, places, and incidents either are the products of the author's imagination or are used fictitiously. Any resemblance to actual persons, living or dead, businesses, companies, events, or locales is entirely coincidental. Well, maybe not entirely...

ISBN (Paperback) 978-0-578-47568-4

ISBN (Ebook) 978-0-578-47569-1

"On some great and glorious day,
the plain folks of the land
will reach their heart's desire at last,
and The White House will be adorned
by a downright moron."

— H.L. Mencken

"Never argue with stupid people.
They will drag you down to their level
and then beat you with experience."

— Mark Twain

ELECTION EVE

Rump rarely reflected. He was finally alone after three rallies, half a round of golf, a staff dinner, and a two-hour appointment with his hair-weave stylist. Wow, big day. And it all ends tomorrow. Or begins. He wondered what it would be like, if he actually won. He had never even considered public service of any kind before this campaign. And the crowds *loved* him. Hey, it could be fun. He called in his campaign manager.

"So, whattaya think?"

"You got it in the bag, Donald."

"Polls say three to four points down."

"The polls are rigged, you've said so yourself many times."

"I don't know."

"You wanna bet?"

"What, if I win I lose?"

"And vice versa."

"I never bet against myself. Bad for business."

"Get some sleep. You've got to get up early to vote."

Right. He wasn't exactly sure where he was supposed to vote, but somebody would tell him. And he had to see the stylist beforehand to eliminate any traces of "bed hair." His wife was probably already asleep in the next room. Lucky. He rarely slept well; his mind was always churning to gain advantage, to game the next play, to trap a possible enemy. Reflection did not occupy much real estate in Donald's brain. Promotion, instinct, a taste for the jugular, these were his trump cards.

But you have to take stock once in a while. How did he get here? How did he defy all the odds, the editorials, and the pundits from both Parties? Some were saying that he was a walking cartoon, nothing more than a haircut atop a small orange hot-air balloon, a self-promoting egomaniacal huckster who was dangerously unfit and unqualified. There were also assessments that could be considered negative.

"Yeah, they can all fry ice," he thought as his mind drifted back sixty years, when his future didn't seem quite so auspicious.

MEET DONNIE

His father had shortened the family name from Rumpelcarpf to avoid embarrassment, but nine-year-old Donnie seemed intent on causing the family a maximum amount anyway. When he wasn't skipping school, he was sent to the principal's office on a regular basis. In fact his classmates coined the phrase for anyone sent to the principal, "Doing a Donnie." He wasn't the sharpest scholar even when he did show up to class. He proudly proclaimed,

"I've never finished a whole book front to back. I'm smart enough to read a little bit here, a little bit there, and know better what the book is about than those losers who wasted time reading the whole thing."

How he ascended grade-to-grade was a mystery. Between his truancy and zilch work ethic, he should have been held back. Where Donnie really excelled was at perfecting the temper tantrum. These often ignited while playing Monopoly.

"I won."

"No you didn't."

"Yes, I did, I have more money."

"You stole the money from the bank."

"NO I DIDN'T, YOU'RE LYING."

"WE SAW YOU TAKE THE EXTRA MONEY."

"NO YOU DIDN'T."

"YES WE DID, YOU'RE A CHEATER. YOU ALWAYS CHEAT."

"OH YEAH? THEN WHY DO YOU PLAY WITH ME?"

"BECAUSE YOU PAY US!"

This exchange continued for another fifteen minutes, when Donnie would throw the board up in the air sending the pieces and dice flying. No problem for him, he knew the maid would clean it up. But it didn't end there. He kept screaming and fulminating for the next two days.

"I'M THE ONLY ONE WHO KNOWS HOW TO PLAY MONOPOLY. THE OTHERS ARE JUST JEALOUS BECAUSE THEY'RE DUMB AND WEAK. THEY LIE ABOUT ME ALL THE TIME BECAUSE I'M TOO SMART FOR THEM. THEY CAN FRY ICE!"

When his ranting got to be too much for his parents, they'd entice him with a crisp $100 bill hooked to a long fishing pole and lure him into a soundproof rubber room. He'd then bounce off the walls like a frantic pinball scoring points. He actually enjoyed this a lot.

The other thing he really enjoyed, perhaps even more than bouncing off the walls, was his lovely cousin Tara. She had clear blue eyes, a winsome smile, and long honey-blond hair. Her hair especially entranced Donnie. He had something of a hairstyle fixation in general and would stare for hours at photos of Frankie Avalon, Bobby Rydell, and Bobby Darin, wishing he could have lush wavy hair like theirs. You see, he had short mossy hair, kind of like a chia pet. He would wear a lot of caps to hide his unattractive clumpy dome.

Tara and he would laugh and frolic together. He would play with her luxurious silky hair, and she would tap his cap yelling, "IS ANYBODY HOME?" And yes, they would frequently play "doctor," after which Donnie would present Tara with a bill for professional services rendered.

INTRODUCING VLADIMIR

Vladimir Poutine was born into a family of KGB agents and apparatchiks during the early days of the Khrushchev regime. The family apartment was quite spacious by Soviet standards, denoting the respect and regard in which The State held papa Poutine. Vladimir was a short child; perhaps he could uncharitably be called scrawny. Which in fact his older brothers did. They often bullied him, throwing him into the Volga saying,

"Пан или пропал" (Sink or swim).

He was a bright lad, and unlike Donnie applied himself in school. But he was often scorned by his peers for his diminutive size. Also unlike Donnie, his father wasn't rich and couldn't afford to buy friends for him. So he was often alone.

In addition to his studies, Vladimir delved into what was known in the '50's as "physical culture." He bought muscle magazines, did weight-training exercises pumping bulk bags of uncut spelt, and performing the squat thrusts and jumping jacks as delineated in the Russian Army Training Manual. He was also fascinated by photos of Johnny Weissmuller as Tarzan, much as Donnie was rapt by the hairstyles of Frankie Avalon and Bobby Rydell. He dreamed of having a rippling chest, bulging biceps, and well-defined deltoids. If he achieved this dominant look, his peers would think twice about demeaning him. He could retaliate in a powerful and decisive manner. Oh yes, he would make them pay who looked down on him.

DONNIE'S PROBLEM

Academic challenges notwithstanding, happy times continued for quite a while, until a serious medical condition occurred. Donnie developed Infantile Alopecia, which meant complete loss of his mossy clumps. There was no baldness in the family, so doctors opined that this was caused by a pituitary imbalance or his frequent cranial collisions from bashing around the rubber room. The prescribed treatment included cracking raw eggs over his head twice a day and vigorously massaging his scalp with a loofah sponge. Donnie hated this routine and would often bolt before the sponge scraped his pate, egg fluid running down his face.

One afternoon after a somewhat vigorous session of "doctor," Tara took a nap under a large tree. Donnie had an idea. He found a large pair of shears and carefully cut off her long blond tresses while she slept. He then folded the silken hair and used an industrial stapler to attach the under layer to his scalp. It didn't really hurt since Donnie had an usually thick skull. He used his mom's Aquanet to fashion a kind of lemon chiffon topping. It didn't look half-bad in his opinion. When Tara awoke she was horrified.

"WHAT HAPPENED TO MY HAIR?"

As soon as she saw Donnie she figured it out and cried. Donnie couldn't understand why. He didn't shave her head; her hair would grow back. He had a good idea and he acted on it. What was the problem? Apparently his father agreed, because he paid Tara some money and asked her not to talk. Of course Tara would never want to play with Donnie ever again. Big deal. There'd be others. The important thing was Donnie looked good!

When Donnie graduated from elementary school there was a celebration. Primarily by the teachers and administration. They fervently hoped they had seen the back of him. There'd be other problem students of course, but Donnie was in a class by himself, whenever he deigned to attend. But as Donnie entered puberty another medical problem presented itself. His body experienced growth spurts, but his brain didn't develop proportionally. Mentally and emotionally he was arrested at the nine-year-old level.

Doctors were at a loss to explain this. Perhaps it was caused by the rubber room behavior, perhaps by the lead staples he punched into his head. Brain scans were ordered, but the detection of actual injury was inconclusive. However, a weird structural malformation within his medial temporal lobe was thought to be a possible key. The area that regulates emotion and empathy was abnormally tiny, and the area that is often linked to ego magnification and distortion was huge.

VLADIMIR WORRIES

Poutine graduated from secondary school with honors at age fifteen. He could no longer be called scrawny, all his exercise and weight lifting changed that, but he was still short. He barely broke the five-foot mark and was surely more diminutive than his peers. He didn't date much. Girls seemed to prefer taller and more conventionally handsome boys. He sometimes felt like ripping off his shirt and proclaiming "Look at this!" But what if he did that, and girls still ignored him?

And there was something else. He also had feelings and stirrings toward boys. It probably started with his adulation of Johnny Weissmuller. He knew that any such glimmer approaching homosexual activity was absolutely forbidden, both officially and by the laws of nature. The Soviet Union imposed very strong penalties on such behavior, and it would ruin his family professionally and emotionally. No, no, no! He knew that discipline and mental focus would keep such degenerate thoughts at bay. He did find pretty girls attractive. If only they would reciprocate. Maybe he could add lifts to his shoes.

In any case, he would concentrate on his studies, and progress through the thicket of the Soviet Intelligence Services to get a good job with the KGB. The right woman would eventually come along, a family would certainly follow, and he would make his father and his Country proud. Oh, yes.

DONNIE AND ROY

Donnie finished his formal schooling, God knows how, and decided to go into the family business real estate. Was his father thrilled. Remember, he had the emotional stability of a belligerent nine-year-old, with an added diagnosis of attention deficit disorder. This explained his low boredom threshold, and his tendency to look into a pocket mirror every few minutes to check out his hair. He did have a kind of personal appeal. With the latest tonsorial technology involving weaves, implants, and rumored serial injections of Himalayan yak blood, his hair did indeed look good!

His father would send him to newly opened Rump Buildings for photo opportunities. He could turn on the charm of a brash nine-year-old and flatter city officials, but there was a problem when photographers would snap a picture. When he smiled, it looked like he was trying to evacuate a particularly obstructive bowel movement.

"It looks like you're taking a dump," his father admonished.

"No it doesn't, I'm just being wry."

"I don't need wry in front of my buildings."

"What do you want me to do?"

"Practice your smile and let me approve it before the next photo. Until then, just stand there."

While Donnie was being an ornament in front of his father's buildings, he did have the chance to meet some influential metropolitan figures, none more so than Roy "King" Kong. Roy was notorious in political and elite social circles. Born an orphan on the lower East Side, he eventually scrapped his way into Columbia's Law School and was admitted to the bar as one of their youngest graduates. He gained renown for suborning the perjury by David Greenberg that helped convict and execute Mabel and Morris Rosensweig for treason. He would later be disbarred for his own perjury, but at this historical moment he was riding high, especially as a darling of the Republican Party. The Rump family often donated to Repub fundraisers, and it was at one of these functions that Donnie and Roy first met.

"Hi Mr. Kong, I'm Donnie Rump."

"Roy, call me Roy. And stop calling yourself Donnie. It makes you sound like a moron. Call yourself Donald."

"Not even Don?"

"No. Too much like a Mafia capo."

"I just want to say how much my whole family admires you, your strength and what you're doing for our country."

"Thank you Donald. The most important thing is to win. These goddamn bleeding-heart Jew liberals, and I'm a Jew so I can say that, crying spilt milk about the Rosensweigs. So what if the Russkies already knew the information they divulged? It set an important precedent for would-be do-gooder, one-worlder liberal pinkoes. You don't fuck around with Roy Kong!"

The most important thing is to win.

You don't fuck around with Roy Kong.

Donnie/Donald would take these pearls of wisdom to heart.

THE CHERNOBYL THING

The Chernobyl Nuclear Power Plant explosion was the worst atomic disaster in history. Chernobyl was near the border of Russia and the Ukraine, and the atomic fallout from the core destruction was over 400 times the radiation emitted from the bomb that leveled Hiroshima. The radioactive dust didn't just stay within the USSR borders, but contaminated its neighbors as well. This was obviously a public relations catastrophe for the Kremlin.

By this time, Poutine was in the thick of the KGB. He was a section chief and was often enlisted to handle sensitive issues that potentially could be embarrassing to The State. He was expert in shutting down journalists and dissent in general that could expose USSR failure. His superior called him in.

"Необходимо обработать эту вещь Чернобыль" (You have to handle this Chernobyl thing).

That's all that was said. Poutine knew what to do. In concert with the Russian Army, over 500 miles of barbed wire were erected, not just around the reactor itself, but around the entire town of Chernobyl, effectively sealing it off from the rest of the world. Nobody in or out. This meant that hundreds, perhaps thousands of people would suffer radiation poisoning, receiving little or no medical attention. But hey, you win some, you lose some. The Soviet reputation for scientific excellence was far more important than the lives of a few thousand people. Poutine's certitude was absolute.

DONALD DEVELOPS

Donald, as he was now known, was promoted from being a Rump Realty hood ornament, to being allowed to initiate some deals himself. The first two didn't go so well. He didn't vet the contractors properly, and they wasted money on nepotistic "consultations and surveying" that went nowhere. The two hundred thousand wasted dollars had to be replenished by his father.

The third deal did work out, and an attractive apartment building was put up in a newly gentrified neighborhood. But a legal violation was in the offing. The word went out to agents that "darkies, brownies and PR's (Puerto Ricans)" who wanted to rent would be coded with a "d" "b" or "p" and refused tenancy based on race. Local journalists got wind of this and a civil rights lawsuit was lodged against the Rump Organization.

Re-enter Roy Kong. By this time he had his own law firm, but still loved sticking it to the liberal do-gooders.

"Goddamn un-American civil rights bullshit! You own a building, you should be able to rent to whoever you want. Who wants to live next to shvartzes and spics anyway? Except other shvartzes and spics. And there goes the neighborhood. We get before a regular jury and we win this thing."

Well, no. Rump had to pay a $250,000 settlement and promise not to discriminate in the future. You win some; you lose some. But during the trial Donald and Roy became closer, almost a surrogate father-son relationship.

"The main thing is never take crap from anybody. Small crap, big crap, it doesn't matter. You counterpunch."

"Counter punch? You mean like hit the kitchen counter?"

Roy just looked him.

"You can't be that dim. No, it's a boxing term. If someone throws a punch at you, metaphorically...do you know what 'metaphorically' means?"

"Sure."

"You drop a cinder block on his head."

"You mean cinder punch."

"You've got one good-looking head of hair there," as Roy tousled it and laughed.

Roy actually felt a physical attraction for Donald;

he had a thing for dumb blondes, and once when they were both drinking, Roy made a sexual advance. When he was rebuffed he said,

"Hey, I don't want you to think I'm queer. I'm not a fag. I just thought you might like to blow me for an experience. Lots of people in this town like blowing me, it's just a mark of respect. I could give you their names, and it would flabbergast you. Do you know what flabbergast means?"

"Sure."

They still spoke occasionally, but Donald thought it wise to put some distance between them.

BUH-BYE USSR

Five years after Chernobyl, the USSR dissolved, and Poutine was out of a job. The nuclear disaster may have hastened its demise, but Mikhail Gorbachev was Chairman at the time and ushered in several liberal reforms that led to the break-up. Many Russians praised him for this, but many bitterly blamed him. And Poutine was among that group.

He eventually was tapped for Russia's Federal Security Bureau, but it was a mere shadow of the vastly more intimidating KGB. For one thing, the new group didn't fight "ideological subversion" which was endemic to the KGB's mandate. There was no longer any ideology to subvert. The glorious Communist Promise was now a dartboard to be punctured and ridiculed. And that chapped Poutine's hide, to put it mildly.

However, he learned to maneuver in the new system. He restrained his nationalist convictions when necessary and expressed more liberal philosophy when useful. But he deeply resented his country's reduced posture on the world stage. It bordered on rage occasionally.

He had an unusual practice to ventilate this resentment and frustration. Once a week he would slip into a silver lamé gown and high heels, pop on a curly wig, and perform Marlene Dietrich classics at a local drag bar. His signature song, "Falling In Love Again," was quite frankly sensational. He was billed as "Valya: Empress of all the Russias" and would often employ a feathered boa to devastating effect. The heels also gave him a stature he lacked in real life.

He had a naturally husky tenor register, and if you closed your eyes, you could almost imagine Marlene/Valya was singing just for you. If future military or government service didn't work out, a career in show business certainly seemed like a possibility.

PAYCHECK

Donald actually did build some structures unencumbered by lawsuits, although many ventures did go bankrupt, but he got bored easily. He loved watching a version of entertainment called "Reality TV." Actually, it was rarely reality and barely TV, but he was fascinated nonetheless. Titles like "Slut Housewives of Sheboygan" and "First Cousins and Their Wacky Kids" often graced the Rump tube. He would repeatedly fob off important business decisions so he could watch more TV.

Then he got a brainstorm. Why couldn't he star on a Reality TV show? He had charm, personality and a great head of hair. He powwowed with some TV execs and came up with a concept: A panel of ambitious, recently displaced business-oriented contestants would audition for a high-paying position with the Rump Organization. The winner would be the one who could most effectively lie, cheat, slander and steal from the other opponents, without seeming to do so. The show would essentially be centered on the job interview as blood sport.

Actual qualifications to do the job would be negligible to winning the position.

The most critical factor to be cast on the panel was physical attractiveness; intelligence and an articulate manner, not so much. In fact Donald was suspicious of such traits. But most importantly, no male contestant could have more stylish hair than him.

Each episode ended with Donald looking a contestant in the eye, shouting "YOU'RE FIRED" and pulling a lever which opened a large trap door under the victim. A plume of smoke would waft upwards replacing the hapless soul. Rump would then sing *"Don't Cry For Me Argentina"* under the closing titles.

As unlikely as it sounds, the show called Paycheck was a smash, especially the end-title song. This was odd since Rump was essentially tone-deaf. His version of the song played on radio stations all over the Country, which helped build the audience. The show improved its ratings week-to-week, until it was often in the top 10. Donald got fan mail for the first time in his life. And he loved it. He especially loved pulling the lever and making people disappear.

Another cool aspect of the show was that it drew a lot of beautiful women into his orbit. Rump had been married several times at this point, but all the unions had failed. The ex-wives had unreasonably expected him to be faithful. Given his tremendous virility and his great-looking head of hair (he often thought of Samson, but wasn't exactly sure who Samson was), no single woman would be enough to satisfy his God-like appetites. He personally hired the women for his staff, most of them in the long, blond-haired innocent mold of his cousin Tara.

And taking a tip from his mentor Kong, he would invite prospective candidates to blow him, as a mark of respect. This could not be construed as employee sexual harassment, because they weren't yet employees. And he did hire a few who refused to fellate him, especially if they had an overbite. So he was legally covered on all sides.

One evening after a session of serial oral sex performed on him by a group known as "Rump's Trollops," (beautiful, specially paid "consultants"), Donald started listening to a radio show called "Disinfowarz." He was rapt by the broadcaster's righteous, virile and almost coherent rhetorical style. This was Rump's introduction to patriotic American and flame-throwing pundit, Alex Clamz.

ALEX CLAMZ

Clamz was actually the product of a botched abortion that left three indentations in the back of his head. He was mocked in school, often called "Bowling Ball" and shunned. This left him isolated and angry. Unlike Rump, he read widely and often cover-to-cover, but he came to an odd conclusion about the basis of what he read. All facts were false. Everything that people assumed was true—that we landed on the moon, that inoculations were critical to fight disease, that the Earth revolved around the sun—were products of liberal indoctrination.

He located a small radio station in Texas and started to broadcast his views to angry, isolated, and aggrieved listeners. And like Rump, his audience grew, even without the off-key singing of Broadway show tunes. The following is a partial transcript of a recent broadcast:

(Announcer: "Defending the republic from enemies real and imagined, it's Alex Clamz.")

"25% of all college students are psychotic; they are actually on anti-psychotic medication. This makes them ripe for the ultra-liberal propaganda that their professors are trying to cram into their heads. Any rational American can plainly see that our Country's future is endangered by elitist college bigmouths who want a Socialist nation. They want to destroy the Free Market, they want to destroy democracy, they want to impregnate your daughters with race-neutral babies to make a one-world, compliant zombie people who will do their bidding. Folks, we've got to fight this! Now listen to me, if your kids are going to college, and personally I'd advise against it, you have to protect them! I suggest you buy a box of Clamz Super Suppositories, guaranteed to clean out the filth from the bottom up. This product is made with the finest all-natural ingredients, guaranteed not to cause diabetes, autism, blood-on-the-brain, epilepsy, or narcolepsy the way other suppositories can. Normally a box of twelve costs $199. But today only, just for my listeners, you can call in with your credit card and the cost will be $150. And we'll pay for shipping and handling! And if you have a friend whose kid is off for socialist indoctrination, buy a box for them for HALF PRICE! Just pay separate shipping and handling."

Rump was impressed with Clamz' salesmanship and marketing savvy. He knew that suppositories cost a couple bucks at most, he often bought them for sex partners, and that Alex could sell them for more than $15 apiece was phenomenal. Donald understood the methodology behind the gouging, or as it is sometimes known, dynamic pricing. Clamz scared his audience with a threatening ideology, and then comforted them with an easy, if expensive remedy. Hmm.

MOTHER RUSSIA

A series of shills and drunks ran his beloved Country for a while, and Poutine bided his time. He wrestled with his conscience about the best way to serve Mother Russia. Should he work his will within the political system by single-handedly dragging his nation out of its second-rate inferiority complex by becoming President? Or should he become an international drag artiste promoting Russian culture? He knew he'd have to make a choice.

"Валя? (Valya?)"

"Кто ты? (Who are you?)"

"Ваша совесть. (Your conscience.)"

"Я похоронил вас в Чернобыле. (I buried you at Chernobyl.)"

"Почти, но не совсем. Ваша страна нуждается вас. (Almost, but not quite. Your Country needs you.)"

"снова влюбиться, никогда не хотел... (*Falling in love again, never wanted to…*)"

"Прекратите это! Вы действительно думаете, 15 минут славы важнее сделать Россию в еликой державой еще раз? (*Stop it! You really think 15 minutes of fame is more important than making Russia a great power again?*)"

"15 минут? (*15 minutes?*)"

"Это американская концепция. (*It's an American concept.*)"

"Никогда не хотел ... (*Never wanted to…*)"

"Будь мужчиной! (*Be a man!*)"

"Что мне делать? (*What am I to do?*)"

"БУДЬТЕ ЧЕЛОВЕК ВЫ КРЕВЕТКИ! (BE A MAN YOU SHRIMP!)"

"не могу помочь. (*Can't Help it.*)"

"ДА, ТЫ МОЖЕШЬ. ПАН ИЛИ ПРОПАЛ! (YES YOU CAN. SINK OR SWIM!)"

THE PROMOTIONAL PRESS CONFERENCE

Every year in Las Vegas, there is a publicity ballyhoo for the TV shows to be broadcast in the upcoming season. The newest programs spend the most money, but returning shows like Paycheck often attend the event to maintain interest and retain some luster. Rump was present every year and loved the attention from entertainment journalists. Since he owned a Vegas casino, the event gave him a chance to trumpet its magnificence as well as cheerlead his reality show.

"Isn't this terrific? I love coming here every year. Vegas really is America, every kind of person coming here to spend money, maybe to win a lot of money, and have a lot of fun in very classy surroundings. Speaking of which, have you been to Rump Castle this trip? We've added a thousand new rooms, a 5000 seat showroom, and the most beautiful hostesses this town has ever seen! Honestly fellas, they'll knock your eyeballs out. I personally vetted each and every one to meet my highest standards. They're all natural, guaranteed. The carpets match the drapes and no artificial flavoring whatsoever."

He expected some laughter at that remark, but received none. He continued,

"So this year on Paycheck, be prepared for some surprises. We have the greatest panel of contestants in history. They will be at each other's throats continuously, and viewers will be on the edge of their seats. In fact we're going to have a health advisory this year before each show, WARNING: IF YOU HAVE ANY HEART OR BLOOD PRESSURE ISSUES DO NOT WATCH THIS PROGRAM. This was on the advice by our legal team to protect us and our advertisers. And by the way, our rates are going up, and companies are clamoring to get onboard! Now questions."

"Donald, there've been accusations that you've made unwanted sexual advances on contestants, staff and others..."

"Look..."

"And that you've paid hush money to women to keep them quiet about your harassment."

"Let me be honest with you. If you want to know the truth, I'll tell you, believe me. I mean honestly, to tell you the truth, you can trust me. In all truthfulness this is all false reporting, believe me. I mean come on, do I look like I need to harass women? I'm rich, I look great, and I'm rich. Believe me, if you want to know the truth, I have to beat them off with a stick, to be honest with you. My dance card is full, to tell you the honest truth, believe me"

"But women have come forward…"

"Losers, disgruntled losers looking for an illegitimate paycheck because they couldn't earn the real Paycheck, if you want to know the truth. And have you seen them? Doggy bow-wows to be honest with you. Truthfully, do you think I'd even be seen with them let alone touch them? I mean, trust me."

"So Donald, what's next? How long will you stay on the show?"

"I don't know, as long as I'm having fun. You know me, if I feel I can't take 100 percent, I'll hand it over to somebody else. But right now we're making a lot of money, giving a huge audience some wonderful television, so what can I tell you? Except, stay tuned."

DONALD MEETS ALEX

"Mr. Rump."

"Mr. Clamz."

"Call me Donald."

"Call me Alex."

And the two gentlemen shook hands in the beautifully appointed private dining room on the top floor of Rump Tower in Manhattan.

"I don't usually eat in digs like this. I'm more a greasy spoon, barbeque rib joint kind of guy. I'm also not a big fan of New York City. Mostly pseudo-intellectuals and queers if you ask me."

"Listen, I appreciate you taking time out of your schedule to come here. And I can get you some tickets for the show Oh Calcutta!, really beautiful nude women live onstage, with a little VIP action backstage just to show you we're not all queer."

"Now we're talking."

"So Alex, the reason I asked you here is, I really admire your broadcasts. And I especially admire the way you rope in ads for your products. How are the suppositories doing?"

"I can't keep up with the demand."

"Really?"

"Swear to God. I'm three months back-ordered. You go to any campus, talk to the kids, I don't mean the pussies at the Ivy-league quagmires, I mean real colleges like Bob Jones, Liberty, and Phoenix, and you'll find they are stuffed full of Clamz Super Suppositories. And student health centers have reported fewer visits and happier clients than ever before."

"Wow."

"Would you like to invest?"

"Maybe. But look, I want to discuss your growing audience base. According to Broadcasting Today your radio share is growing exponentially. I mean you're not doing Limbaugh numbers, but all he sells are "Dittohead" merchandise. You've got a very nice blend of commerce and politics that could be very powerful. Ever think about running for office?"

"Never. I hate politicians. Even the ones I kind of like. First they have to castrate themselves to get enough votes to win, and I never wanted to be a eunuch. Second, I could never tolerate the bullshit that comes with the process. Look, I'm all in favor of democracy, but it takes too goddamn long to get anything done! This is my show, I say what I want, when I want to. Period. And as you know, a lot of people respond. I can have more influence outside the system than in."

"Okay. Well I *am* thinking about it."

"You want to be a politician? Wouldn't that be a serious pay cut for you?"

"Not necessarily..."

"Wouldn't you have to stop running all your businesses? Conflict of interest stuff?"

"That doesn't apply for the President."

Alex just looked at him for several seconds in silence.

"It doesn't?"

"Nope, my lawyers have been checking it out. The President is the one office where there is no such thing as conflict of interest. So I guess I have no choice."

"You're planning to run for President?"

"Well I ain't gonna start in the mailroom, I'll tell you that. I'm starting to get bored with my TV show, and I figure I can leverage my popularity for a greater purpose. So what do you think?"

"I'll tell you Donald...I like your show, I like your style, and I like your hair. Is it yours?"

"You bet. You want some? Next time I get a trim I'll send you some. You can staple it to that dome of yours."

"Swell, but let me give you a little advice. If you're serious about gathering real political power, you need to read Hitler's 'Mein Kampf' and Mussolini's 'My Autobiography'. I know, they were bad guys, but they knew how to mobilize public opinion. They really did."

"Alex, this could be the beginning of a beautiful friendship."

READING, HERE AND THERE

Donald still didn't have the patience to actually read a whole book, but he could occasionally read an entire page, here and there. He kept copies of Clamz' suggestions by his bedside and tucked in for inspiration before nodding off. There were several Hitlerisms that made a strong impression:

What luck for rulers that men do not think.

"That's true, I don't spend a lot of time thinking."

The great masses of the people will more easily fall victim to a big lie than to a small one.

"I can buy that, go big or go home."

The art of leadership consists in consolidating the attention of the people against a single enemy and taking care that nothing will split up that attention.

"That makes sense. Nothing unifies a Country like war against an enemy."

It is not truth that matters, but victory.

"I could have written that one myself."

Rump also watched footage of Hitler and Mussolini together at a conference. Or what he thought was footage. It was actually part of Chaplin's film "The Great Dictator." Donald was particularly impressed with Mussolini's physically intimidating presence, even though it was comedian Jack Oakie doing a rather good impersonation. Donald jutted his chin out, folded his arms across his chest and rocked his feet side-to-side a la Mussolini (Oakie).

"It is not the truth that is important, but victory," he declaimed to the mirror.

He felt good. Real good. And he had much better-looking hair than Benito, who of course had none.

POUTINE GOES BIG

Vladimir sensed the time was right. His countrymen were fed up with Gorbachev era reforms. They were fed up with being considered a second-rate "regional influence" consisting of mostly sloppy drunks and depressive losers. They were also offended by the West's "cultural imperialism" promoting tolerance and diversity of thought. These had little place in Mother Russia. One nation, one people! In fact "tolerance and diversity" had a demoralizing effect, a feminizing effect. Even though he hadn't thrown away his silver lamé gown and heels, he loathed the feminization of society. He loathed sensitivity, homosexuality, non-Christian religions, the free press, yoga, and essentially, everything the West was promoting to further its notion of liberal democracy. What rubbish!

He was appointed Vice-President by the then-current Russian President under the condition that

Poutine would grant a full pardon for any misdeeds, aka embezzlements, that might be discovered. For history buffs, think of the Nixon-Ford transaction in the '70's. He soon ascended to the Presidency and consolidated all power in his new position. He wanted to be the leader of a "New World Order of Nationalism and Traditionalism." And those who wouldn't follow would be left behind. Often in a ditch or the river. An amazing number of journalists and opponents died under suspicious circumstances during this time. 132 to be exact. They were poisoned, drowned, shot, stabbed, hacked, garroted, run off the road, fell out of windows, slipped off roofs, and other even more exotic terminations. And none of the perpetrators were ever convicted, or even found.

When asked about this Poutine said, "Что я могу сказатьвам? Человекумирает. (What can I tell you? People die.)"

THE RUMP MOVEMENT BEGINS

Donald descended a golden staircase, stepped onto a golden chariot being led by six beautiful blondes draped in golden centurion garb, traveled twenty yards to a golden podium and spoke to an assembled audience of 800 or so. Many were Rump Organization employees required to attend, and others were paid by a field team to show up. When he arrived at the podium, a great cheer erupted from the crowd.

"Thank you my friends, my fans, and close associates. Let me be honest with you, we're in trouble. I don't mean we at Rump International, I mean we in America. We don't win anymore! And when say "we", I mean you. I win all the time. More businessmen want "RUMP" on their buildings than any other name in the world, believe me. When I say America is losing, we're losing jobs to Mexico, Japan, China, Vietnam, Indonesia, Estonia. ESTONIA. Little Estonia makes the dust filters for air conditioners that used to be made right here. We're losing the war on drugs, the war on crime, the war on terrorism, and protecting our National border integrity. More Americans have been killed by illegal immigrant terrorists on drugs after crossing our non-existent defenseless borders than at any other time in history, if you want to know the truth. And it's time that stops. Don't you think it's time for that to stop? (crowd cheers). To be honest with you I'm fed up, aren't you fed up?" (bigger cheer).

"That's why I want to hitch my track record of success to America's future, and that's why today, right now, I'm announcing I will be running for President of the United States."

A fifty-foot long banner fell from the ceiling with golden block letters outlined in black border reading: **RUMP FOR PRESIDENT**

"And ladies and gentlemen we are not going to be 'the patsy' anymore, the fall-guy, the weak guy bending over and taking it from every other country in the world. No more 'mister nice guy.' We are going to stand up and be strong. We may be a little prickly at times, a little irritating to countries who take advantage of us. And they take advantage of us all the time, believe me. And so our campaign motto is going to be: *"MAKE AMERICA GRATE AGAIN!"*

With that, the offstage orchestra played the familiar opening chords, and Rump launched into *"Don't Cry For Me Argentina."*

THE CLAMZ ENDORSEMENT

"All of you in the front lines of the Disinfowarz, you listen to me and you listen good. By now you know that Donald Rump is running for President. You know him from his TV show, you may know him from his buildings, but I know him as a man. I've met with him. I've broken bread with him, and I can tell you he is worthy of your support. No, I'll go further. You should join the Rump team and fight for him! He doesn't need your money, but if he appears in a town near you, bring twenty friends and make a loud noise. He shares your values, he shares your heritage, and he will fight against the moral corruption and decay that is eating away at our Country's vitals. For many decades now, politicians of both parties have been like maggots in the White House. No, more like termites eating away at our foundation with their effete little teeth, sucking at the sugar tit of our Nation's bounty without giving anything but termite dung in return."

"Speaking of which, we just got a fresh shipment of Clamz Super Suppositories just in time for college finals. And if you order right now, get a ten percent discount off a three-box trifecta. And I want to assure you that we will have Rump on this show in the very near future."

Donald was appreciative of the endorsement and bought 100 palettes worth of Super Suppositories to pass out as future party favors or holiday gifts. He wondered if they'd be appropriate to distribute at political rallies, but frankly he didn't want to cut into Clamz' profit margin.

Rump started to assemble his campaign public relations staff. The group known informally as "Rump's Trollops" from his TV show would serve as his talk show surrogates. They were all lovely and had facial surgery that enforced a broad smiling countenance at all times. These were Babette, Candy, Kylie, Ginger, Amber, Trixie and Mona, and while their names sounded like seasoned adult film actresses, there was no commercial evidence to support this.

RUMP ON THE STUMP

Donald loved zipping around in his private jet. He seemed to have boundless energy to meet fans and possible supporters. Wherever he arrived, people would start chanting, after being prompted by some paid plants, "Make America Grate Again!"

"Yes, yes, I love this. That's what we're going to do, Make America Grate Again! No more 'mister nice-guy.' If you want to know the truth, I'll be honest with you. We are thought of as weak everywhere. Nobody respects us anymore, believe me. They laugh at us! Every country in the world thinks we're a joke. Well, when I'm President, the joke's on them, believe me. We are going to build a wall, a big beautiful wall, around the entire perimeter of our Country. That's right. Nobody will sneak into our Country anywhere without our knowing about it!"

"And what about the mess we're in at home. The

crime rate is sky-high, crimes of violence are higher than they've ever been, if you want to know the truth. One out of three people will be mugged or murdered if I'm not elected. And that's not just me talking, if you want to know the honest truth. Just listen to Alex Clamz! Do you like Alex Clamz? (wild cheering). We'll bring back jobs, we'll stop violent crime, we're going to lower everyone's taxes, we're going to build new roads and factories, and every citizen will get one free night in a Rump Hotel during the first year after I'm elected, what do you think about that? (even wilder cheering) Just remember, I alone can do this, trust me."

(Announcer: "Attention, this is a Disinforwarz special. Presidential candidate Donald Rump and Alex Clamz go head-to-head for the first time. Don't you DARE change this channel. Listening to this program could be critical for our nation's survival. And now, America's prize-fighter for freedom, liberty and the right to fight the thought police, ALEX CLAMZ.")

—canned applause and whistles—

"Folks, you know I have been the only one who will tell you the truth. And you know I can't be bought off. Well now, there's another one. And he may be our last best hope to save America. It is my pleasure to introduce Donald D. Rump, candidate for President of the United States. Donald, welcome."

"Alex, thank you, and I want to say what an honor for me to be here so your audience can get to know me and what I stand for, believe me."

"And what do you stand for?"

"I stand for strength, and respect, and telling the truth about the rotten state our Country is in, to be perfectly honest with you. I believe in everything you've been saying on your show for years. Our citizens live in fear, fear that they'll lose their jobs to foreigners, fear that they'll be robbed or killed by foreigners, fear that their way of life is forever threatened by everybody! Foreigners, the government, the media, everybody. And look, you know that the chances are one-in-three listeners will be violently attacked or even murdered in their lifetime, believe me."

"Absolutely, Donald. These are incontestable facts the fake media will never present to you. They'd call it "fear-mongering" or "bad science" or whatever crap they choose. But when they quote one-in-two men will get cancer, and one-in three women will get cancer, and we have to stop smoking, eat less sugar and lose weight, then the New York Times and Washington Post stand up and salute! And that's not fear-mongering? We use the same metrics and demographics they do, and chances are very good that you'll be violently mugged or killed before you die. And speaking of that, you really need to buy a Clamz Special Semi-Automatic for your personal protection. Only $800, made from the finest burnished metal alloy, unbreakable under normal use. It holds a forty-round clip, and comes with either a feather-light or moderate trigger pull, accurate up to twenty-five feet. And if you buy a second gun for a loved one, we'll include a half-box of Super Suppositories for only ten bucks. You can't beat it!"

RUMP IN RUSSIA (PART ONE)

After the Soviet Union's collapse, Rump International started alliances with Russian oligarchs. The business environment was free-market capitalism without regulation, and the prospect of unfettered wealth was mouth-watering to Rump. He also salivated in the presence of young beautiful women from the former Eastern bloc, and in fact married several of them. In addition to marriages, his deals included luxury apartment buildings, luxury car franchises, luxury gourmet food emporia, and a brothel (with luxury red velour upholstery). Once Poutine became President, the oligarchs mysteriously died, and Rump was compelled to deal with him personally. Their first meeting occurred ten years before Donald's dive into the maelstrom of Presidential politics.

"Mr. President, it is a pleasure to finally meet with you. I've always enjoyed my trips to your Country, but my Russian is limited, basically 'comrade,' 'da,' and 'vodka.' Do you have a translator?"

"Mr. Donald Rump, I can speak English perfectly fine. I usually prefer not to, in deference to my people's choice."

"Ah, you're a cagey one, aren't you."

"Yes, I recently fought a tiger in a cage and won. Now the reason I ask you here is to tell you we must re-negotiate our deals that mutually benefit your company and our Country."

"Go on."

"You must realize that your former Russian partners are no longer available. Now I know that in addition to the 60-40 split in your favor, you created a shell company that skims an extra ten percent off the grosses of all Rump Russian properties."

"Your Mr. Turnbulgakov is a good man."

"I don't mind the skimming, that is to be expected. But the split will be reversed. 70-30 in our favor. This is non-negotiable."

"Everything is negotiable Mr. President."

"Not this, Mr. Donald. We are fed up with America and Americans taking advantage of us. You will accept my terms or we will simply take your properties. You read newspapers, yes?"

"Occasionally."

"Then you know we have terminated several co-ventures between our two Countries. The reason we're allowing you a generous thirty percent is that your name does have some value to us, but..."

"Thirty-five percent."

"100% of a smaller pot is still more advantageous..."

"Thirty-four percent."

"Thirty-one."

"Thirty-three."

"Thirty-two."

"And a half!"

Vladimir just looked at him, and smiled slightly.

"Done. Now let's go to the Svetskaya Brothel to ensure that quality control is being maintained."

Donald loved Russian prostitutes. They were usually younger, prettier and wilder than their American counterparts. They were also willing to be sprayed with Lysol first, to accommodate Rump's obsessive germophobia. American prosties usually refused, bitching about stinging or some other such nonsense. Donald especially looked forward to hot, germ-free sex and side orders of the most delicious caviar, often eaten right off the girls' bodies. He wasn't opposed to mess, just germs. This was from Poutine's private stash: not too salty, not too fishy, just the perfect burst of flavor when spread over a woman's nipples.

What Rump didn't know was that all his brothel

fun was being videotaped and preserved. This wasn't just because Poutine was a perv; it was simply standard procedure to videotape all American behavior everywhere. Since image was so important to Donald, had he known, he might have been more assiduous about cleaning the caviar from between his teeth.

STAYNE BANNAN

Stayne Bannan, CEO of BrightFog news, came to Rump's attention via Alex Clamz. Clamz and Bannan shared the same basic world view, that beneath apparent "facts and truth" was a conspiracy to camouflage a tissue of lies. BrightFog often fielded exclusive stories through Clamz' microphone to reach a wider audience. These included:

"The government plans to abolish the second amendment and forcibly remove your guns by armed Democrat appointees."

"Democrats are planning to forcibly sterilize white women to increase the percentage of minority voters in the future."

"Newborns will soon be implanted with a chip that will allow the government to track them forever."

"The National Institutes of Health will soon offer

$1000 to every white woman willing to have an abortion." Etc.

Alex thought that Stayne would be a valuable asset on the Rump team. Unlike others in this story, Bannan came from a warm, loving middle-class family. He did well in school and had many friends. Unfortunately, a rabid weasel nipped him at age twelve while he was shooting pigeons for fun. The rabies wasn't discovered until late in its incubation, and doctors thought he wouldn't survive. But he did. Miraculously, he seemed to fully recover except for one odd residual effect. Occasionally he would foam at the mouth for no reason. Sometimes this would occur during a hissy fit, but sometimes just while eating corn flakes. The foaming moments would pass, and no one made much of it.

"Mr. Rump."

"Mr. Bannan. Alex thinks the world of you, and I think the world of him. So what can you do for me?"

"Donald, I have the inside lane to the kind of press you'll need to win this thing. In addition to BrightFog, I have contacts at Fox, Drudge, and forty of the most revered blogs on the internet. My words, or rather your words can reach into the minds of millions of people and make them your willing supplicants."

"Supplicants?"

"Followers, folks who'll do anything you say."

"That sounds good."

"More to the point, I can give you information to really scare people into voting for you. It's not enough to parrot Alex; you need some original ideas of your own. And I can give them to you."

MALLORY CLAXTON

Rump's campaign rolled on. Chants of "Make America Grate Again!" greeted him wherever he appeared. And the crowds were getting larger, with fewer paid attendees necessary. Folks loved having their photo taken with him, but whenever he tried to smile, his father's observation of yore still pertained. It looked like he was trying to evacuate his bowels.

Mallory Claxton was a formidable woman. She was a Secretary of State, a two-term senator, and a former First Lady. She was always "top-of-the-class," conscientious, curious, and genuinely civic minded, devoting much of her life to public service. In other words, she was everything that Rump was not. But also unlike Rump, she was not telegenic, nor broadly popular.

Quite a few found her shrill, unappealing, and far too "uppity" for her own good. And her hair style could generously be described as frumpy. But for good or ill, she was positioned to be Rump's main opponent. She would often strategize with her friend and close counselor Raina Aberdeen.

"Mallory, you discount Rump's appeal at your peril. *Paycheck* gave him an enormous platform and visibility. You and I may not have liked the show, but millions did. It got tremendous ratings for most of its seasons."

"So how does that qualify him to be President? That he can draw eyeballs and sing 'Don't Cry For Me Argentina' off-key?"

"That was also a huge hit. God, you couldn't turn on your car radio without hearing the damn thing played repeatedly on short rotation."

"And that ridiculous slogan, 'Make America Grate Again?' What the fuck is that? What undiluted bullshit is he peddling?"

"Whatever he's peddling, people are buying it. I have boots on the ground at his rallies, and folks love that trope. They think America has been too soft and needs to 'grate' again."

"So what should be our slogan be, 'Shred 'em all, we're the best?'"

"Mallory..."

"Stick it to them before they stick it to us?"

"I don't think the electorate would buy that from you."

The slogan Mallory and her team developed was "Mallory Makes Sense." This was to draw the obvious distinction between her and Rump. Some thought the motto wasn't punchy enough, but then again Mallory probably never studied Mein Kampf.

THE DEBATE

"In this corner, weighing in at 138 pounds, former First Lady, two-term senator, and Secretary of State, Mallory Claxton."

She entered from the left in a smart, cream-colored pants suit and took her place at her podium.

"And in this corner, weighing in at 325 pounds, the President of Rump International and sole owner of its more than 500 subsidiaries, Donald D. Rump."

He entered from the right in an Italian tailored dark suit over a white shirt and red tie, and took his place at his podium.

"Ladies and gentlemen, we expect a dirty fight to justify the high cost of commercial time we're charging. Thirty million people may be watching, so be aware that every word and gesture will be dissected and parsed *ad nauseam* by pundits from now until doomsday. And now, LET'S GET READY TO RUMBLE!"

"I'd like to set some ground rules. I'll call her Madame Secretary, if she calls me President Rump."

—cheering and applause—

"Cute. I think I'll call you Donnie, because that's what you called yourself until you were twenty-six."

"Ok Mallie. First, that's a lie; I never called myself Donnie. Second I think we should talk about what really concerns the American people, to be honest with you."

"Agreed Donnie, and what affects the American people most is the quality of leadership, the steady hand that can lead this Country into the future, a future that benefits everyone equally."

—applause and cheering—

"First, you are dead wrong, believe me. What affects Americans most, are the crime, the poverty, and the massive unemployment rate that is ravaging the average person's pocketbook, if you want to know the truth."

"Ok Donnie, let's take a look at crime, poverty and unemployment. They are at their lowest levels in twenty years. Those are the facts. Period."

"You can take your facts, and shove them up your valise. You talk to the average American, which I do all the time, and you'll find he's frightened, unemployed or under-employed, and can't pay his bills, if you want to know the truth."

The Haircut Who Would Be King 73

"Now Donnie, I talk to average Americans every day, in fact they elected me twice to the Senate. You've never been elected to anything. Maybe you were appointed the King of Rumpworld by your rich daddy, but aside from that, you know nothing about governance."

—applause—

"I've created thousands of jobs, how many have you created? The people who know 'governance' have put America on the road to bankruptcy."

"Bankruptcy, now that's something you DO have direct knowledge about. How many of your companies have gone bankrupt? How many people have lost jobs in your companies? How many workers have you stiffed by refusing to pay them? How much wealth have you lost for your investors?"

"You're changing the subject Mallie, HOW MANY JOBS HAVE YOU EVER CREATED? EVEN ONE? Maybe you created some jobs for your staff, but for the average American, zip-a-de-doodah. When I'm elected, people will have good paying jobs again. They'll have their dignity again. MAKE AMERICA GRATE AGAIN!"

—cheering—

"Careful Donnie, you're turning red. Do you have your blood pressure meds available? You don't want to have a seizure onstage."

"I don't have seizures lady, I give them! You're the

one who almost fell on the tarmac last week, not me. My doctor signed off that I'm in perfect health."

"That phony doctor's report you gave to the press was total bull. He said that *you* wrote 'He'll be the healthiest President in history,' and he just signed it while you were waiting in the car."

"That's a total lie made up by the fake media. And let's face it, when you have a hot flash, you might start World War III, if you want to know the truth."

"Look Donnie, you're known to be a sexist pig misogynist, you have seventeen lawsuits against you for harassment. Now don't go proving it with your big mouth."

"You have the big mouth, not me."

"Eighty-six percent of respondents in a poll said you have exactly the wrong temperament to be President."

"I have the best temperament of any candidate in history, believe me. I have a winning temperament. It doesn't matter what kind of rigged poll you quote."

"People think you're unqualified, unfit, and a clear and present danger to the welfare of our nation."

"And people think you're weak, low-energy, stale, and attractive as a day-old corpse."

A bell rang offstage.

"And that's the end of round one. Stay tuned for round two after our commercial break"

—wild cheering, applause and foot stomping—

RUMP IN RUSSIA (PART TWO)

"Comrade Donald," as Poutine embraced him warmly in the Gold Room of The Kremlin.

"Mr. President, did you catch my performance opposite Claxton?"

"Da, you mopped the floor with her. Of course she is just a wretched woman. I wonder how you would have fared against a formidable man. An American version of me, perhaps."

"Vladimir, I *am* the American version of you."

And both men chuckled.

"Donald, I want you to meet someone."

A slight blond figure, male, approached and extended his hand.

"This is Julian Aashlonge, founder of Wakidrips, the powerful cyber hacking network."

"Mr. Aashlonge, I've heard about you. You can crack into any computer and seize its contents, apparently.

Aren't you under house arrest somewhere for something?"

"Well yes and no. Our good friend Vladimir has a lot of leverage which allows me to travel somewhat freely here."

"I wanted you two to meet under my protection, because I think this could be an advantageous alliance for all of us."

Vladimir poured an incredibly expensive cognac and continued.

"Julian hates Mallory almost as much as you do, and he can help you win the election."

"What's your beef?"

"Mallory insisted I be tried for rape; she put pressure on these bogus courts to persecute me."

"Don't you mean prosecute?"

"She persecutes me so they'll prosecute me. I mean how can you rape a prostitute anyway?"

"*She persecutes to prosecute, to prosecute for prostitute,*" Vladimir enunciated. "Say that ten times fast, gentlemen."

They tried with varying degrees of success, and laughed as they drank their cognac.

"So here's my offer, I will hack into Mallory's computer as well as the upper echelon of the Democratic Party, and dump all their e-mails into the public domain. I'll release it everywhere all at once. If you like, I'll let you vet the material first."

"I don't have the time for that, believe me."

"Ok, I promise you there'll be a trove of embarrassing material. There always is. And once it's released, you can disparage Claxton's lack of effective security. I mean if she can't secure her computer, how can she secure the Country?"

"Oooh, I like this."

"In exchange, you pay me one million Euros through Vladimir."

"Let's make it a million dollars."

"I'm not running a charity, Donald."

"I can probably do the hacking without you."

"Not as effectively, and if the fingerprints can be traced back to you, you're finished."

"Three-quarters of a million."

"Vladimir has to take his cut as well."

"800,000."

"900,000."

"850,000."

"Done."

And all three shook hands.

"Now gentlemen, let's all repair to Svetskaya for a little relaxation. Donald, I have a supply of that excellent caviar you so enjoy, and Julian, I have a beautiful young blonde ready and willing to be raped for your pleasure."

The three men arrived at the brothel and were treated like the royalty that they truly were. Of course, videotape covered everything.

THE WAKIDRIPS DUMP

Mallory Claxton was afraid she'd be implicated in the suicide of a former chief of staff...

The Former Secretary of State acknowledges her mistakes led to the death of embassy personnel...

The Claxton charity foundation funneled millions to off-shore accounts to hide illegal profiteering...

Mallory called Rump supporters "a bucket of scumbags who eat their own boogers" at a fundraiser...

Mallory's lesbian lover from college stays in touch and advises...

These and 20,000 other e-mail "headlines" were dumped by Aashlonge within two weeks of the Russian deal. Mallory responded.

"First, I need to tell you that my computer and many others within the Democratic National Committee have been hacked and material has been stolen. Second, we don't know who is responsible, but it seems like a foreign power is involved based on the initial investigation into the cyber fingerprints. Third, no one has vetted the dump for accuracy, and I can tell you that many of the releases I've seen are categorically false and malicious. Now we have to ask, who benefits from this? And who had been slapped with new lawsuits regarding sexual harassment of contestants from his TV show, just before this dump of illegally acquired lies? You think this is a coincidence? I call on Donald Rump to denounce this illegal invasion into our American electoral system and demand it stop."

And Rump responded

"First, I'm not denouncing anything. I think we should all welcome any information about secretive Mallory Claxton. Second, if she feels something revealed is false, it's up to her to prove it. That's the American way. And third and most important, if she can't protect her own computer, how can she protect the American public? I ask you, in all honesty, HOW CAN SHE PROTECT THE REST OF US??"

Aashlonge continued to drip embarrassing and inflammatory e-mails about Claxton and her campaign, but national polls showed Mallory was ahead in the race. This drove Rump a little crazy. Polls were like ratings, and his TV show was always tops in the ratings. He vented at a rally.

"My friends, let me be honest with you. The polls are rigged, if you want to know the truth. And if Russia really is involved in the hacking, more power to them. It's time Mallory Claxton's crimes came out in the open, don't you agree? (cheering) And I'll be honest with you, when I'm elected President, she'll be locked up for treason, murder, theft and underage lesbianism with a minor, believe me. MAKE AMERICA GRATE AGAIN, and if you want to know the truth, I'm going to grate on Mallory Claxton like nobody's business. Trust me."

All well and good, and red meat for his supporters. But there was one problem. Russia had never been mentioned as a source of the hacking. Mallory used the term "a foreign power." Journalists noticed the unexplained attribution, and asked the question,

"Why did Rump mention Russia in the hacking and encourage them?"

Rump and Bannan conferred about the gaffe.

"Donald, you've got to check yourself a little more."

"People like it when I speak off the cuff. They like it when I sound authentic."

"This isn't about authentic, this is about giving journalists a lead to investigate possible ties between you and Russia."

"First, nobody believes 'journalists' anymore, and second they won't find anything. Poutine will deny any connection and blame it on the liberal press."

"But *you're* the one who mentioned Russia, not the journalists."

"Stayne, something you've got to learn if we're

going to work together. I don't like being criticized. If I make a mistake, it's your job to cover it up. I read BrightFog, and you print all kinds of confusing and contradictory stuff. And I think that's great! Just do what you need to do."

MARYANNE CURTSY

The sexual harassment lawsuits against Rump to which Mallory alluded in the debate were piling up. Donald's lawyers tried having them dismissed, but to date none were. He needed an attractive articulate woman to speak on his behalf. He thought about one of Rump's Trollops, some were almost articulate, but their talents were better deployed elsewhere.

Bannan suggested Maryanne Curtsy as the best person for the job. She had been a Republican operative for two decades, and she was smart, loyal, soft-spoken and well liked on both sides of the congressional aisle. She was also easy on the eyes, and with her long blond hair she reminded Donald of you-know-who.

"May I call you Maryanne?"

"Sure Donald. So Stayne briefed me, but I need to hear from you what you're expecting."

"Maryanne, I need women to vote for me. These bullshit lawsuits, absolutely baseless by the way, I never had to force myself on any woman, believe me. In fact I've had to extricate myself from women who wanted to compromise *me*, if you want to know the truth. Anyway, these lawsuits are impacting my negatives. Now the cases won't be tried before the election, but who knows what's going to squeeze in over the transom. I need you to put out the fires and tell American womanhood that they're safe voting for Rump."

Maryanne decided to come onboard for two main reasons. The pay was great, and she had a little bit of a daddy thing. She was raised a Catholic, but her parents divorced anyway when she was three years old. By the time she joined the Rumpwagon, she had been through several husbands and was raising four kids on her own.

She found that a large part of her job was "translating" Rump. For instance he would say,

"Most immigrants have no reason for being here and do not respect our way of life. They do not wish us well believe me, and all atrocities committed on our soil over the past ten years were committed by illegal aliens, if you want to know the truth."

And she would translate "What Donald means is that we need to screen people coming into our Country to make sure they're not terrorists."

Rump: "We're going build a huge wall around the entire perimeter of America to protect our citizens, and the United Nations will pay for it. I mean if the Chinese could build a Great Wall, I know how to build one better than the Chinese, believe me."

Curtsy: "What Donald means is we need to have obstacles to be sure terrorists don't come into our Country."

Rump: "Birth control makes women ugly and those who have abortions will have to be punished, to be honest with you. Women have to learn to respect life, just like everybody else."

Curtsy: "He means we need to be sure people don't pretend to be women, when in fact they're terrorists."

Rump: "We have to disband the fake media. Make it easier to sue them for libel and remove their credentials. The Second Amendment is more important than the First Amendment, believe me."

Curtsy: "Donald is clear that terrorists cannot, and will not somehow get credentials as journalists."

It got a lot easier to translate Rump as time went on. It was as reflexive as breathing.

NAUGHTY RUMP

The video didn't exactly squeeze in over the transom. It was actually delivered through the regular mail and arrived at the Original Cable Network (OCN) with the handwritten instruction "Open This ASAP." The image was grainy, but in focus. A man, apparently naked, was sitting on a bed with a leggy blond, also naked, face down across his lap. He had a ping-pong paddle in his hand.

"Oh yes, daddy. Spank me."

"I'll spank you, Tara." (whack)

"Tara? Isn't that from *Gone With The Wind*?"

"Shut up, Tara." (whack)

"Oooh, grab me by the pussy."

"I'll grab you by the pussy..."

His hand shot down between her legs as he delivered another whack.

"Yes, faster."

He complied and she squirmed rhythmically. The patter and activity continued thus for several minutes. The man's head may have tilted downward, but the voice was certainly recognizable and the haircut unmistakable.

Portions of the tape were broadcast by OCN, and then "borrowed" by every TV station on the planet. The woman's buttocks were covered by the somewhat witty caption, RUMP ENDER? The Rump campaign went into full "Code Red" mobilization.

Maryanne was the first to respond publicly.

"The sleazy video making the rounds of the biased, ultra-liberal media, is an abominable attempt to smear the reputation of Donald D. Rump. He categorically denies any memory of the event purportedly depicting him on tape. He feels the visual is probably photo-shopped and the audio is an impersonation. He feels the Claxton campaign is behind this vicious leak, and frankly this kind of slimeball tactic has no place in presidential politics."

The Claxton campaign replied quickly.

"Mallory had no knowledge of this tape and was certainly not its source. But the issue is not a sleazy video, it is the sleazy person *on* the video that counts, and it is clearly Donald D. Rump. He proves conclusively that he is unfit to be President, that he is a latter day Marquis de Sade, and that frankly he should step off the ticket. Period."

Technology experts were brought in to examine

the tape, and the consensus was, no evidence of tampering or photo-shopping. In fact when the image was enlarged, the furniture and fixtures in the room were consistent with those found in the New York Rump International Hotel.

Maryanne responded to the experts' report.

"Mr. Rump continues to deny any memory of an event that may or may not have occurred in one of his hotels or somewhere else. Experts can disagree about video duplication, just as they do about climate change. But Donald wants you to know, that if it is hypothetically him, what is happening in that room is a totally legal exchange between two consenting adults. And I think you'll agree, it takes real courage for a candidate to say that. The kind of courage our Country needs to lead it out of the darkness we're currently in."

Billboards started popping up around the Country showing a large ping-pong paddle and the phrase "Is This Really For You?" above it, and MALLORY MAKES SENSE underneath.

Rump was livid when he met with Bannan and Curtsy.

"GODDAMN IT, I WANT TO BURN THOSE BILLBOARDS DOWN! JUST THROW SOME GASOLINE ON THEM AND LIGHT 'EM UP. I'M BEING MADE A LAUGHING STOCK, AND I AM NOT A LAUGHING STOCK!"

Bannan was foaming at the mouth.

"WE CAN DO THIS. I HAVE OPERATIVES IN EVERY STATE WHO CAN DO THIS. I'M SURE CLAMZ HAS PEOPLE TOO. WE CAN USE SELECTIVE EXPLOSIVES. IT'S MORE EFFICIENT THAN GASOLINE AND LESS CHANCE OF COLLATERAL DAMAGE."

Maryanne handed Bannan a handkerchief.

"Jesus Stayne, wipe your mouth. You can't destroy the billboards. I'm sure Claxton has volunteers watching them..."

"NOT EVERY MINUTE..."

"...and somebody's going to get hurt. And it's going to get back to us. You can't be seen instigating destruction of private property. You're the champion of free enterprise. It'll lose us votes."

"WELL WHAT DO YOU SUGGEST WE *CAN* DO MISS CURTSY? YOU'RE TELLING US WHAT WE CAN'T DO, WHAT CAN WE DO?"

"For a start, calm down and count to ten. Now Donald, I need to know, that *was* a consensual act wasn't it? She's not going to come out of the woodwork and claim she was coerced, or it was quid pro quo for a job or something?"

"I don't think so."

"Did she ask to be spanked? Or was it your idea..."

"Jesus Maryanne, I honestly don't remember her, if you want to know the truth. I've had dozens of women like that. Maybe I took her to Le Cirque for dinner or something"

"Was she a pro?"

"I don't think so. Most of them wouldn't know about the Tara/*Gone With The Wind* connection."

"Ok. Stayne, can you get something on Mallory? Maybe some lesbian footage with an underage girl?"

"I'll work on it," wiping off the remaining spittle from his mouth.

"Now don't you go photo-shopping footage from *Candy Stripers in Trouble*, or something. I mean it!"

"Ok."

"Absent that, we let it fade. And believe me, it will."

FALLOUT

However, it didn't. Rump continued to sink in the polls. He repeatedly said that the polls were rigged, but TV news crews interviewed potential voters about Donald's paddle problem.

"This joker wants to lead our Country? Let him host 'America's Most Disgusting Home Videos.'"

"I couldn't look my daughter in the eye if I voted for him."

"I won't vote for Mallory, but I can't vote for him. Not now."

"Somebody should paddle Rump. Often."

"If he wants public office, let him start as dogcatcher and work his way up."

"GODDAMN IT, YOU SAID IT WOULD FADE MARYANNE, IT'S NOT FADING. **DOGCATCHER??** I WANT TO KEEP THAT TAPE AND FIND OUT

WHO THAT CLOWN IS. IF I'M ELECTED I'M GOING TO MAKE HIS LIFE A LIVING HELL!!"

"Stayne, have you found any lesbian footage on Mallory?"

"Not yet."

"Ok, I'm going to drill down into one of those Wakidrips, the one about possible complicity with those embassy deaths when she was Secretary of State. I've got friends in State and Justice."

American Ambassador Warren Miller and three of his staff were murdered in Abuja, Nigeria by the terrorist group *Beaucoup de Haram* (literally translated as "much sinful garbage") in 2012. Mallory was Secretary of State at the time and was scrutinized for possible dereliction of duty in failing to protect the embassy. She endured weeks of bi-partisan congressional hearings into the Abuja massacre and was fully exonerated. Of course none of this deterred the Rump campaign. They broadcast their message through the Clamz microphone.

(Announcer: "Attention, exposing Mallory Claxton's criminal crimes regarding the Nigerian Ambassador's murder on Disinfowarz. Here's your peerless fighter for God, truth and the American Way, Alex Clamz.")

"Folks, we have breaking news about Mallory's State Department malfeasance from the Rump campaign. And this is a helluva lot more important than ping-pong paddles, believe me. Mallory Claxton knew the Nigerian embassy was going to be attacked *one week* before the tragedy. That's called accessory before the fact. If she is elected President, she will be impeached immediately after the inauguration, because, listen to me, accessory to murder is a high crime, forget the misdemeanor. AND we have evidence that Mallory perjured herself before the congressional committee. That's also an impeachable offense. So at the very least, if you want to avoid a constitutional crises, vote Rump! And don't forget to buy a box of Clamz Super Suppositories, because in these troubled times, we can all use a little help."

The Claxton Campaign responded.

"Hopefully none of you look to Disinforwarz for anything more than Saturday matinee horror-movie entertainment. Remember, they said that American agents destroyed the World Trade Center, that we never landed on the moon, and that Marilyn Monroe was murdered by Bobby Kennedy who was then murdered by Clem Skudnik, Marilyn's secret husband at the end of her life.

"Don't forget that Clamz is shilling for Rump, and Rump is shilling for Clamz and his suppositories. And they are both covered in the product that suppositories stimulate. Mallory Claxton mourned the death of her friend Warren Miller and did everything she could to prevent this tragedy."

THE FINAL LAP

The last two weeks before the election, things *really* got nasty in campaign shenanigans. Fist fights broke out during Rump rallies, egged on by Rump. If a protestor dared show up at one of these rallies, supporters would pummel the hapless soul, with Donald cheering from the sidelines.

"That's right, take him out. Beat the crap out of him. If you get arrested, I'll pay for your defense." (He never did.)

During Mallory events, people would chant,

"Rump's retarded, Rump's retarded," until some mental health professionals interceded stating this was unfair to the "mentally handicapped," which was the preferred term anyway.

To recap each candidate's summary argument:

"My friends let me paint two American futures for you. The first is a Country that welcomes our neighbors and realizes our strength is in supporting each other. This is the Country that Emma Lazarus extolled with her words at the base of the Statue of Liberty 'Give me your tired, your poor, your huddled masses yearning to breathe free.' The second is a Country where we live in constant fear of everything, where we look for a strong man like Hitler, or Mussolini, or Stalin to save us from fears that are largely being stoked by a pathologically damaged candidate. Donald Rump has a serious medical problem that his phony-baloney gastroenterologist, you know, that homeless derelict who signed 'He'll be the healthiest President in history,' should have discovered. Rump's medical problem involves his digestive tract being wired backwards, so that everything flows in reverse. And that's why he talks out of his butt, and nothing but crap comes out of his mouth! Please think about that on election day. Remember, MALLORY MAKES SENSE!"

And,

"Folks, you know what's at stake here. To be honest with you, I may be the last chance to save America. You know I'm very smart, and a very successful businessman. I didn't get there by luck. I don't need this job, but I'm willing to share my expertise to pull our nation out of the sludge it's been in for decades, the quicksand that *both* Parties have been shoveling, if you want to know the truth. I'm not beholden to either Party. I will serve you. I will be beholden to you, your needs, your safety, your right to a decent good-paying job. Remember that the fake media is in the tank for Mallory; they've been rigging the polls in her favor for months. Prove them wrong! Remember what the *real* media, I mean BrightFog, The National Enquirer, and Clamz have been saying, 'a vote for Mallory is a vote for a Constitutional Crisis and impeachment!' You know that crime is up, and jobs are down. Wall Street is up, and Main Street is down. The elites are up, and the regular people are down. All that's going to change when I'm elected, believe me. And remember, every citizen will get a free night in a Rump hotel up to a year after I take office. Let's MAKE AMERICA GRATE AGAIN!"

THE ELECTION

Rump won.

THE DAY AFTER

Donald D. Rump would become the next President of The United States, with the lowest percentage of the popular vote in American history. He received fewer votes than the previous Republican Presidential nominee, who *lost* the election four years earlier. He actually received three million fewer votes than Mallory Claxton.

Go democracy! But he did win the majority of electoral votes, and that's what counts in America, to the confusion and consternation of the rest of the world.

The first leader to call Rump was Vladimir Poutine.

"Mr. President-elect, may I offer my heartiest congratulations on your spectacular win."

"Mr. President, thank you so much, and I look forward to meeting with you soon."

"Please expect a shipment of our most excellent

caviar. Tell your adjutants to keep the caviar in its protective casing chilled at ten degrees centigrade."

"Thank you Mr. President."

"And Donald, I will be sending you by diplomatic pouch, a list of possible candidates for consideration to fill your cabinet positions. Some you may know, some you may not. But let's talk. I look forward to working very closely with you, guiding international policies and positions for our mutual benefit. We will establish our own World Order. *Nastrovia*, President Rump."

The major polls and news outlets did somersaults and *mea culpae* to explain how their predictions went so awry: they over-counted cell phones, they under-counted cell phones, people were embarrassed to say they'd vote for Rump, they over estimated the enthusiasm for Claxton, the Wakidrips were more influential than expected, the ever-popular sunspot factor or maybe there was a mind-control element found in Clamz' suppositories. Or perhaps people just really wanted that free night in a luxury hotel.

Rump looked over Poutine's suggestions for staffing and conferred with Bannan and Curtsy. Stayne actually had dealings with Poutine in the past and recognized some of the energy titans and financial barons on the list. In fact several of them supped together at different times in The Kremlin. They were to a man impressed with the caviar and the Svetskaya entertainment.

Bannan confirmed Poutine's recommendations for key positions in State, The Treasury, and National Security. Donald looked these over for a few minutes and agreed with the choices. All were extraordinarily wealthy with longstanding ties to Wall Street. What was that populist trope that Rump used in his final speech? *"Wall Street is up, Main Street is down. The elites are up, the regular people are down. I will be beholden only to you"*

Well... As Hitler said,

"What luck for rulers that men do not think."

THE INAUGURATION

Rump took the oath of office to "preserve, protect and defend the Constitution of the United States of America," and that was that. Rump was the Prez. Many performers who often play at inaugural events found they were busy and couldn't attend. The reasons ranged from last minute family reunions, to emergency cosmetic surgeries, to piñata stuffing for several children's birthday parties.

Prominent among those who *did* perform were The All-Girl Sheboygan Bratwurst Choir singing a peppy *The Best Things in Life Are Free*, Ted Nugent singing a virile new composition *Do It 'Til It Bleeds*, and the Manafort Mandolin Trio playing a haunting mash-up of *Moscow Nights* and *Katyusha*. The wacky kids from the "First Cousins" reality show tried to do some comic acrobatic shtick with middling results. The two brothers, heads down, ran at each other at full speed, and knocked each other out. Donald seemed to enjoy the show immensely.

Of course he knew it was customary to deliver an inaugural speech, but he wanted to send a message that his was to be a different kind of Presidency. So he gave the speech three days later. He knew it was important to unite the Country and bring people together.

"My fellow Americans, I know it's important to unite the Country and bring people together. But that was some terrific election, don't you think? I really ate Mallory's lunch. Wow! And we had the largest audience for any inauguration in history. We won by the largest electoral landslide in recent memory. And we would have won the popular vote by huge numbers if illegal aliens had been prohibited from voting. We're going to make sure that never happens again, believe me. We're going to build up the Defense Department, and we're going to build that wall around our Country, I can tell you that. And the United Nations will pay for it! It's the least they can do. Now some people have asked, 'How are we going to get to the beach? Will there still be a beach, or will the wall replace it?' First, there will still be a beach, I promise you, and second, every citizen will get a permanent pass to enter the door through the wall to access the beach.

"Now I want to say 'thank you' to everyone who voted for me, and for those of you who didn't, don't worry. We're all allowed to make mistakes. I'm your

President too, and you'll change, believe me. Now is the time for all of us to pull together and move forward. But you must admit, that was one world-class electoral upset, all the pundits and news organizations with egg on their face. And you wonder why I call it fake news. They got it wrong because they get *you*, the real Americans wrong.

"But that's going to change, trust me. We are going to have a tremendous administration with the best people ever assembled to help me govern the Country. And I want you to remember one thing. Unlike politicians, I will never lie to you. Believe me. And now, as a special treat, perhaps for the last time, *Don't Cry For Me Argentina,*" and he launched into a full-throated a cappella rendition that probably delighted many of his supporters.

HARD WORK

This President business was harder and more complex than Donald thought it would be. He didn't understand the concept of "checks and balances" on executive power. He certainly didn't have to deal with them as the president of his company, and he was probably absent from school when The Constitution was studied. He needed to think things through. He needed to understand why his ratings were dropping. He needed another rubber room in which he could bounce around.

His contacts in the construction business would prove useful in this regard. During the wee hours of the morning over several weeks, builders worked feverishly to devise a deluxe padded room near the White House gym to Rump's specifications. The expenditure was fobbed off to "miscellaneous expenses". Once it was finished Donald spent an hour a day bouncing off the walls. He found it mentally useful and reasonably good physical exercise as well. He had gained thirty pounds since inauguration and thought this activity might help shed some of the weight and lower his blood pressure in the bargain. Of course he was now about 250 pounds heavier than the last time he pinballed from wall to wall, so his speed of collision was somewhat reduced. And now there were other ways to reduce stress.

"Okay, I'm going to play some golf," he addressed Stayne and Maryanne.

"Hold it Mr. President. North Korea just tested an intercontinental ballistic missile, intel has new evidence that Iran may be breaking its nuclear enrichment agreement, Turkey has just arrested 2000 people who may have been involved in an attempted coup, and 5000 bodies have been found in a Nigerian mass grave attributed to Beaucoup de Haram."

"So?"

"It's not even the weekend."

"And?"

"People may think you're not putting in a full day."

"Okay. Stayne, blame all of the current situations on the previous administration, and that America will personally hold all those countries responsible for their actions."

"Couple things, Beaucoup de Haram is not part of the Nigerian Government. They're Islamic terrorists that Nigeria has been fighting…"

"Not very well I'd say..."

"...and you don't want to piss off Turkey. You have several Bosphorus resort permits at stake."

"Ok, you figure it out, but make me look good."

Rump needed lots of downtime from his Presidential duties. Every weekend he would hop on the Presidential Jet to visit one of his worldwide resort properties, at taxpayers' expense. Most previous Presidents would repair to Camp David in Maryland for a little R&R; it was a beautiful highly-secure compound with all the amenities, but Rump didn't own Camp David. Since there was no conflict of interest for a President, Donald could charge The Treasury for his expenses, which effectively would be paid to the Rump Corporation. Sweet. The tab was about three million per junket. Of course he planned to make huge cuts in discretionary spending: education, the arts, environmental protection, labor protection, civil rights protection, election protection and medical research. So his three million travel price tag per trip shouldn't spike the deficit too much.

THE CREDIBILITY PROBLEM

Donald always had a shaky relationship with the truth, but for some reason, people expected that he would firm it up once he was President. "I will never lie to you, believe me," he said during his inauguration. News outlets reported there were four quick lies in that very speech:

1) We had the largest audience for any inauguration in history. It fell far short compared with the previous President's inauguration.

2) We won by the largest electoral landslide in recent memory. Unless you have the memory of a flea, you'd know that Rump's predecessor won by a much larger margin.

3) We would have won the popular vote by huge numbers if illegal aliens had been prohibited from voting. Illegal aliens **were** prohibited from voting, and there was no evidence to the contrary.

4) I will never lie to you, believe me. And OJ is still looking for his wife's killer.

But these were relatively minor lies. Of course Hitler said,

"The great masses of the people will more easily fall victim to a big lie than to a small one."

Hmmm, what plausible big lie could Donald use to coalesce public opinion? Let's face it, public opinion was not exactly in Rump's favor at this time. Oh, the Paycheck fans were solidly in his pocket, but the public at large, well....

"OCN has the latest Gallup Poll numbers regarding the public's favorability of Rump at this early point in his Presidency, and they are not positive. Only 36% think he's doing a good job, 56% think he's doing badly, 8% aren't sure. These are the lowest favorability ratings for any President at the start of his administration in the history of public opinion polls. The numbers divide most dramatically between the well educated and the poorly educated. 85% of those with college degrees weigh in negatively; 90% of high school dropouts think he's just swell."

A week later, Rump went out to rally his base, even though he had won the election and there was no legislation that he was cheerleading.

"I want to tell you, I love the poorly educated! Did you read those rigged polls? (boos) I am here to serve you, not the polls or pundits! (cheers) We're going to

Make America Grate Again, believe me. (louder cheers) We're going to bring back all the manufacturing jobs we've lost over the past twenty years. We're going to open up all the closed coal mines. We're going to roll back regulations that cut jobs and make employers spend more time on paperwork than hiring good Americans. (cheers and stomping) We're going to show the fake media. We're going to show the pundits. We're going to show the elites that we mean business, and business is good for America. (wild cheering, chants of 'Rump, Rump. Rump') Now listen, everybody wants their free night at one of my hotels, and I understand that, they are great hotels. But you're blowing up my reservation lines! We've had to install extra fiber optics to handle the load. And people who want to pay for reservations can't get through! So please, I ask you, be patient. Every citizen will get their free night, believe me, but we've got to find a way to work this out."

Newspapers and newscasters questioned whether it was even remotely possible to offer every citizen a free night in a Rump hotel; of course they questioned a lot of Rump's numbers. A few of his dubious quotes involved crime, illegal voting, immigrant mischief, jobs, his business success, his waistline, even the number of floors in his structures (apparently he "removed" fifteen floors from one of his apartments, literally jumping from 22 to 37 because people would pay more for living at a higher level). Donald's cries of the "fake media" persecuting him still resonated with some people, but a number of his voters were having buyers' remorse. What big lie could reverse his fortunes?

OPERATION UNICORN

Rump convened a special committee called "Operation Unicorn" to come up with a really potent, cool big lie that could capture the whole Country. Of course Bannan, Curtsy and Clamz were chosen to serve along with Agents X, Y, and Z who had ties to Russian disinformation campaigns. They would meet at least once a week to brainstorm. Several possibilities for a grand deception were batted about, but none received sufficient traction within the group.

In the meantime his favorability rating hovered in the low-thirties among the general public. And editorial pages were having a field day. Some of the more incendiary opinions were titled, "AMERICA GRATES ON RUMP," "RUMP in a HOLE," and, "I CALL HIM DONNIE DOUCHEBAG, WITH **MORE** THAN DUE RESPECT." The highlight of that editorial written by Max Punch is as follows:

"Some folks think it's disrespectful to call the President of The United States of America a douchebag. Even though he has historically low approval ratings and is manifestly unfit and unqualified to be dogcatcher let alone President, people often use the phrase *with all due respect, blah blah blah...* meaning 'I don't want to seem to insult him, so I'll pay some deference to civility, but...' Well, I call Donnie Rump a douchebag because he's earned the insult honestly, and he has destroyed all norms of civility long ago. People have asked me to explain why I say 'with *more* than due respect,' so I will. A douchebag actually performs a useful function competently."

"GODDAMN IT, IS THIS THE SAME ASSWIPE WHO CALLED ME A DOGCATCHER DURING THE CAMPAIGN?"

"No sir, this one's a journalist."

"WELL, PULL HIS CREDENTIALS."

"I don't believe he attends the press briefings."

"WELL PULL 'EM ANYWAY! AND WHAT'S GOING ON WITH THAT FIRST DOGCATCHER CLOWN? HAS HE BEEN UNCOVERED? YOU KEPT THAT TAPE AS I WANTED, RIGHT?"

"Yes sir."

"WELL, GET THE FBI ON IT. IDENTIKIT OR VOICE RECOGNITION OR WHATEVER THE HELL THEY USE. I WANT HIS ASS IN A SLING."

"He might not be in any criminal data base, sir."

"JUST DO IT! THE FBI WORKS FOR ME, RIGHT?

I KNOW WHAT THEY DO, I USED TO WATCH THE SHOW ON TV."

With continual attacks on Rump's credibility and competence, Operation Unicorn took on an extra urgency.

"Ok, so what do you have for me this week?"

"An asteroid is on a collision course with Earth. It's due to hit by the end of the year and will end all life as we know it," Clamz offered.

"Naw, too many people saw the movie. And astrophysical bigshots will deny it."

"I can get some scientists to confirm it, guaranteed."

"The ones who said we never landed on the moon? Next."

"Alien creatures from Area 51 have come back to life and are eating everything in their way as they move toward Las Vegas. Residents will be given cyanide capsules to assure a painless death."

"Somebody besides Alex."

"Democrats are being investigated for plotting a coup against this Administration, involving potential murder and theft of the nuclear codes. House arrests are being issued to prominent members of Congress," Stayne offered, a trace of foam on his lips.

"Is that actually true?" Rump asked with alarm.

"I think I can make it work," Bannan assured, wiping some saliva that dripped onto his shirt. "Give me the greenlight, and I'll improvise off the old Watergate playbook. In fact some of the kids of the original burglars have done business with me. Very skillful and loyal. AND if they're caught, they can do accents to make them seem like immigrants."

"Wait a minute," said Maryanne trying to inject a little sanity. "There are people around who still remember Watergate. And you do recall how that eventually played out, right? We don't want to plant evidence that can eventually be traced back to us, which we then have to cover up, and it's the Nixon follies all over again."

"Okay Ms. Curtsy, so what have you got for me?"

"I'm working on something, but unlike everybody else, I want to offer an idea that's fully baked. In the meantime, I want Agents X, Y, and Z to fly to Detroit, Chicago, and Denver."

"Why?"

"To research municipal water supplies, aquifers, sediment and safety precautions."

THE BIG LIE

During the early days of the Rump Presidency, Poutine was relatively satisfied. Donald had taken his suggestions for positions in the State, Treasury and National Security departments. Vladimir also approved the Commerce Secretary, even though he didn't personally offer the recommendation. He hoped the new Administration would tilt American policy more favorably toward Russian ambitions. He and Donald had an understanding; they both knew that the masses yearned to be led by a strong hand.

However, Poutine didn't expect the American media would be so virulently anti-Rump. After all, American media virtually made Rump an honored household guest with the popularity of Paycheck. It was a mutually gratifying love affair for many years. So the swift reversal of affection caught Vladimir up short.

The major news outlets were also implying that

Russia was having undue influence on Rump's decision making. The word *collusion* was frequently being used to describe the Rump-Poutine-Aashlonge activity during the campaign, and even during his presidency. Rump was extremely defensive about this and would insert the phrase "No Collusion" often as a non-sequitur into all of his press releases.

This was occasionally confusing, to wit:

"Unemployment has reached an all-time low, and everybody knows there's been no collusion whatsoever!"

"I am totally opposed to white supremacy, and I don't even know what the Ku Klux Klan is. But I do know there is no collusion!"

"The First Lady and I are totally on the same page regarding social issues, but there has never been any collusion."

Finally many newspaper editorials agreed, echoing the statement, "There is absolutely no evidence of collusion between this President and known reality whatsoever. We also cannot confirm there is ongoing contact between his brain and his mouth."

Collusion aside, connections had not yet been established between Donald's cabinet choices and Poutine's preferences, but investigations were ongoing. Vladimir realized he might have to re-think the relationship. Thankfully he had all that Svetskaya brothel footage of Rump's frolics to use as possible leverage for future negotiations.

At 9:00pm EST on a Monday all television and radio broadcasting was interrupted.

"THIS IS THE HOMELAND SECURITY EMERGENCY COMMUNICATIONS SYSTEM. WE HAVE A CRITICAL STATEMENT FROM THE PRESIDENT OF THE UNITED STATES, PRESIDENT DONALD D. RUMP."

Rump appeared at his desk looking very presidential and spoke directly into the camera.

"My fellow Americans. It has come to my attention that we face a National Crisis of historic proportions. The drinking water supply of at least three American cities has been massively poisoned by foreign entities. The cities are Detroit, Chicago, and Denver, and other cities have apparently been targeted as well. Over 1000 citizens have been taken ill, and many have died from drinking this toxic water. We have classified information that Islamic extremist groups are responsible for this horrific crime against our people. We know that at least 10,000 foreign agents may be involved, therefore; we are closing our borders to ALL non-US citizens for the next ninety days, subject to further extension. This may cause some inconvenience for visitors, but my job is to protect our Country and its people first. All reservoirs and water treatment plants will be patrolled by armed National Guard soldiers. Do not approach without proper credentials. Their orders are 'shoot to kill.' The Surgeon General's advice is to buy all drinking water from recognized vendors, but if you must drink water from the public supply, boil it first for two minutes and sift any sediment out before drinking. Do not use drinking fountains anywhere. This is a tremendous challenge for our Country; perhaps the greatest challenge America has ever faced. God willing we will all come through this national emergency united and stronger. Good night and good luck."

Needless to say, in the following days there was a run on bottled water all over the Country, particularly in Detroit, Chicago and Denver. Lines were long and tempers short. Fights broke out in stores, and folks got hurt. In fact ten people were shot to death in "stand your ground" states due to water possession disputes. Rump made no speeches that might to calm the situation and alleviate the panic. Actually, the Unicorn team devised the story precisely to incite this kind of agitation.

The truth behind the lie that "foreigners are poisoning Americans" is that water *was* being contaminated, but by aging delivery systems and delinquent companies. Lead and rust from pipes were the main culprit, as well as chemical runoff from manufacturing plants illegally dumping waste into feeder rivers. News reports had investigated the Detroit pollution for years, but Republican governance in Michigan had quashed any action to remediate the danger because of the cost, not to mention the corrupt payments from the offending businesses to the outstretched hands of politicians.

There were some cases of water-borne illnesses in other cities, but these were common enteric viruses, not nefarious "poisons." And yes, some did die, but these were people with weakened immune systems anyway. There was no evidence of a specifically deposited contaminant. Rump's assertion that foreign entities had massively poisoned the water supply was backed only by his word and classified intelligence that could not be divulged.

There was also collateral harm that Donald had not envisioned. Several mosques around the nation were firebombed with worshippers burned inside.

Men and women perceived to wear Muslim garb were regularly assaulted for no reason. Clerics of all faiths pleaded for tolerance and decency in the absence of any such appeals from The White House. Donald may not have been the sharpest student in the world, but he seemed to have absorbed one of Adolf's major lessons:

"The art of leadership consists in consolidating the attention of the people against a single enemy and taking care that nothing will split up that attention."

MIXED RESULTS

During this time of phony national crisis, Rump's poll numbers actually did rise into the mid-50's. The Nation rallied around the President's actions to "protect our Country and its people first." Of course there were news outlets demanding to see the proof of foreign sabotage and Islamic terrorist links, but the White House insisted that any leaks of classified information would harm national security.

Congressional efforts to start an independent investigation were quashed by the Republican majority.

(Announcer: ATTENTION, THIS IS A DISINFOWARZ BREAKING ALERT: AMERICA UNDER ATTACK DAY 63, HERE'S YOUR RELIABLE PATRIOTIC SENTINEL, ALEX CLAMZ.)

"Okay, first the good news. It seems that deaths from the poisoned water supply have leveled off. But this is not the time to be complacent. Traitorous fake-news reporters are saying there never was an alien terrorist attack on our drinking water, and they insist President Rump release classified intelligence to prove that there was a coordinated attack executed by Islamic terrorists on our soil. And congressional Democrats are in cahoots with them, can you believe that? Write your congressman today and demand that the immigrant travel ban be extended. Write them that it's more important to keep State Secrets than it is to put American lives at risk. And write them to help subsidize the poor so they can buy Clamz Super Suppositories, because even if you're not drinking polluted water, constipation is no joke, believe me.

"Now listen, you mustn't physically attack people who look Muslim. Folks who listen to me have been arrested for assault saying this broadcast encourages such behavior. *That's a lie!* I'm saying, *don't* hit them! But you can scream at them. That's protected speech. So if you see anyone who looks fishy, scream whatever you want! And don't forget, buy those extra suppositories, because a rainy day is coming, believe me."

On the other hand, the immigrant ban had a negative impact on several businesses, particularly agriculture, patient care, and tourism. Workers with perfectly legal permits and visas, who had contracts, who had employers expecting their labor, were all foiled. And there was no date certain when they would get permission to enter the Country. Many of these businesses were natural Rump constituents, and they were pissed off. They had supported his candidacy, and now they felt betrayed.

There was also an event that developed into a National Tragedy during this time.

Two brothers were playing near a reservoir just outside Denver. They were of the age where dares, double-dares, and cries of "chicken" were taunts to challenge the fortitude of the other. They goaded each other sufficiently to climb the fence, and within minutes after they descended on the other side, they were shot to death.

They were white, photogenic and a genuine pain-in-the-ass to the Rump regime.

"GODDAMN IT, COULDN'T THE SOLDIERS SEE THEY WERE JUST KIDS?"

"You gave the Guard the order to shoot-to-kill, remember? They could have been Islamic midgets. You warned everybody about this in your speech."

"YEAH, BUT WE'RE GONNA GET REAMED IF IT'S REVEALED THAT YOU CAME UP WITH THE PLAN, MARYANNE."

"Donald, nothing's going to come out. When it comes to National Security, you hold all the cards. You can claim Executive Privilege if necessary."

"I always thought that sounded sleazy; I said so when Nixon did it. And look what happened to him, remember?"

"We can also look into the background of the soldiers. Maybe they weren't properly trained during the previous Administration."

"Hmm...."

"It's okay Donald. You'll send a personal note of condolence to the parents and smooth things over."

"But Maryanne..."

"Shhh, you need to relax. Listen, do you want me to bring in a Trollop to blow you? Would that help?"

"Yeah, maybe."

Trixie flounced in, it was her shift, and with comfy velvet kneepads she assumed the position. And she certainly performed a useful function with a high degree of competence.

GREET THE MESS

Donald wrote the note to the parents of the dead boys but committed a critical error. He finished the letter with "your sons died defending this Country that they loved, and so they died as heroes." He forgot that these were just a couple of kids, not soldiers protecting the water supply. Needless to say, the parents were not heartened by the Presidential condolence. In fact they were furious and shared their anger with the press. The Sunday talk shows were on fire.

"Good morning, welcome to *Greet The Mess*. Let's get right to our panel: Kelly Blank—Rump supporter, Raina Aberdeen—Former Claxton advisor, Rich Ladle—Republican Strategist, and Max Punch—The Times editorial writer. Let's start with a clip of the parents of the two boys who were killed at the Denver Reservoir just a few days ago."

A tall thin man and his wife faced the camera, the

man with a letter in his hand trembling slightly. The man spoke,

"This is the letter that President Rump sent us after our sons were shot to death by members of the National Guard. It is a short letter and ends with, 'Your sons died defending this Country that they loved...and so they died as heroes.' Our sons were just a couple of kids playing. They weren't heroes, and we have a President who either can't tell the difference, or just doesn't care. We voted for Rump, and we are ashamed to have such a thoughtless, careless man leading our Country."

"Okay Kelly, your response."

"First, this was a tragedy, no question. But the boys knew they shouldn't be playing near the reservoir, and they certainly knew or should have known not to climb the fence. Frankly, their parents bear some responsibility as well. They should have..."

"Wait a second Kelly," Raina interrupted. "You're avoiding the main issue here, that we have a President who doesn't know what he's doing. He writes a letter, he doesn't speak off the cuff, theoretically takes time to write the letter and then confuses two little boys for the soldiers who killed them. How does that happen? What kind of mental process allows that?"

"Raina, that's not fair," Rich weighed in. "We should have some compassion for those soldiers. You didn't show the clip where they expressed deep regret. They are heartbroken. They were relieved from duty, but they were just following orders."

"Wow, 'just following orders?' That's an unfortunate reference from the past. You're deflecting and distracting from Rump's thought process or lack thereof. I repeat, what was he thinking when he wrote to the parents saying their sons died as heroes?"

"Max, your thoughts? After all you wrote an editorial way back comparing the President to a...feminine device used for internal cleansing..."

"With more than due respect."

"... and I suspect you are not sympathetic to Rump apologists..."

"Look, I think all Americans grieve with the parents of those two little boys and have sympathy for the soldiers. They are all essentially victims of the petty tyrant occupying The White House. Someone asked about his mental process. He has the mental process of a sea slug, which leads to his governing policy of Rumpology. Rumpology means doing or saying anything you want without being tethered to facts or concerned about consequences..."

"Max, you're being..."

"Rich, let me finish. There are rumblings that this whole business of Islamic terrorist water poisoning is a hoax. Rump won't reveal details of the plot to anyone because it's classified. Independent labs have examined samples from multiple water sources, and no pathogens have been found. Just industrial runoff and lead. And of course Republicans have prevented a congressional investigation. So all we have essentially is Rump's word! You know, just like his assertion that illegal lesbian pedophiles gave Mallory the popular vote. Well la-di-da, let's all take that to the bank. Impeachment is being mentioned in some congressional quarters. It needs to escalate from a 'mention' to a steady drumbeat. If it's true that Rump just made it all up to boost his poll numbers, then it's more than an impeachable offense. It's accessory to murder."

RUMP FIGHTS BACK

"GODDAMN IT, I WANT TO SUE THAT COCKSUCKER FOR SLANDER. HE CALLED ME A MURDERER."

"Calm down Donald."

"AND I DIDN'T CALL THE LESBIANS PEDOPHILES, I CALLED MALLORY…"

"Do you want Trixie to blow you?"

"NO! I WANT THAT COCKSUCKER FINISHED. FIRST HE CALLS ME A DOGCATCHER, THEN A DOUCHEBAG THEN A MURDERER? POUTINE WOULD KNOW WHAT TO DO WITH HIM. AT LEAST I CAN SUE HIM."

"No you can't."

"I'VE SUED PEOPLE ALL MY LIFE. I'M PRESIDENT, GODDAMN IT."

"Donald, it's because you're President that you

can't sue. First, he didn't call you a murderer. He said, '*If* it's true that he made it all up...'"

"I DIDN'T MAKE IT ALL UP, *YOU* MADE IT ALL UP!"

"Donald, don't be a douchebag, pardon my French. Second, no President in history has ever sued a journalist. Not even Nixon."

"Well I'm different, people like that."

"It will re-emphasize the claim that you're thin-skinned and petty. It will just fan the flames, believe me."

"Fine, whatever you say Maryanne," as he stamped his foot.

The Rump bump in favorability vanished after his failed condolence attempt. In fact the polls dropped to either side of thirty percent, depending on the week. He was losing ground with much of his base: white males, mainstream Republicans, and high school dropouts. Yes, even the poorly educated were getting off the Rumpwagon.

"Vladimir, it's Donald."

"Yes Mr. President, I know. You called me on our exclusive hotline."

"I need Aashlonge. I need more Wakidrips released."

"From where? He released everything he had to help you."

"Does he still have taps into high-level Democrat computers?"

"Probably."

"I need some internet chatter that Democrats are plotting against me. That they are secretly trying to stage a coup to replace me. I think you would call this plotting *active measures*."

"Are they?"

"There's no proof that they're not."

"Mr. President, have you thought this through? I know your approval ratings are down..."

"Only according to the rigged polls. Not all, not all..."

"Do you plan to arrest these 'disloyal Democrats?'"

"I'll scope out the choices with my team. Right now I have to mobilize public opinion, to redirect anger against me to the Democrats. Wakidrips worked before the election, there's no reason why it shouldn't work now."

"I'll talk to Julian. But it might be better to amplify what you want through our bot network rather than Aashlonge."

"Bot network?"

"It can replicate information tens of thousands of times and transmit directly to e-mails and websites from what seems like an official verified source. All it takes are a few keystrokes."

"Cool. I wish we could do that."

"I believe you can Mr. President. You should talk to your CIA."

"Well, many of them are disloyal. Is this bot stuff really effective?"

"Did you hear that many Alaskans want to sell Alaska back to us? A petition 'Alaska Back To Russia' was started and linked to a prominent Anchorage conservative blog. 30,000 people have signed so far."

"30,000? Who started the petition?"

"A fellow named *Yogi Bear* with a Macedonian IP address. But he actually has an office here in The Kremlin. Effective, wouldn't you say?"

POUTINE'S DILEMMA

Vladimir was having problems of his own during this time. 1000 dissidents congregated in Red Square to protest against government corruption and murdered opposition members. A bomb was thrown into a St. Petersburg subway killing seventeen and wounding thirty others. A second bomb was found in another subway station, but thankfully deactivated. And perhaps most critically, his popularity dropped from 82% to 64%. While this rating would have put Rump on cloud nine, Poutine felt it was like a slap in the face with a frozen herring.

He dispersed the Red Square malcontents with water cannons, and many were arrested for "protesting without a government license." He appeared on Russian television, bare-chested, and promised that law and order would be restored on the streets. The Russian media, essentially controlled by Poutine, praised his swift strong response to the civil unrest, but they were quiet as to the subway bombing. There had been no arrests or even attribution of responsibility.

Many Russian citizens were also starting to complain about consumer goods that were increasingly unavailable due to economic sanctions. These were leveled by the previous American administration after Russia's incursion into the Ukraine and taking Crimea for its own. For a while, Poutine used the sanctions as a point of national pride.

"Мы будем ходить с гордостью и процветать независимо от незаконные американские усилия чтобы наказать нас как чрезмерной родителя. (We will walk proudly and thrive regardless of the illegitimate American efforts to punish us like an overweening parent.)"

And his countrymen agreed. For a while.

"Mr. President."

"Please, call me Donald."

"Donald, we have the bot messages ready to go. They will infiltrate the Democrats' computers at the same time they enter the Fox news, BrightFog, and Drudge websites, in addition to several sites we've masked under various names."

"Excellent Vladimir."

"Now I need something in return."

"How much?"

"Not money. I need you to rescind the economic

sanctions, You know they're unfair, and our people are hurting."

"I'm not sure I know how to do that."

"Ask your people, they can help you."

"Ok, and listen, America sends its sympathy on the subway bombing. Have you found them yet?"

"Thank you Donald, we will. And we'll release the bot network once we hear your announcement that the sanctions will end."

RUMP'S DILEMMA

It was just the two men in the Oval Office.

"Stayne, we have a problem. I didn't want Maryanne here because she's too conciliatory."

"Shoot."

"I've spoken to Vladimir. He's willing to spread your idea that Democrats are plotting to overthrow me. Something called a "bot network"; it'll send tens of thousands of internet messages taken from what look like Dem computers. News outlets will pick it up, and then we can arrest the plotters and declare martial law."

"Cool."

"Only problem is, I have to rescind the economic sanctions first. Can I do that by executive order?"

"I don't think so. You need to have congressional consent, and with your approval ratings AND the chatter that Russia influenced your Cabinet choices..."

"Yeah, the ratings are bullshit, and those pussies in Congress won't do the right thing. They only care about getting re-elected. So what's the next step?"

"Okay. You might not like this, but... Your hypothetical ratings dump started in the aftermath of the water infiltration deal: no evidence, the condolence letter and all that crap, right?"

"So?"

"We throw Maryanne under the bus. The water supply poisoning story *was* her idea. You trusted her reputation from her decades working with the Republican Party. You had no way of knowing she would conspire to create a National Crisis just to cover up her own mistakes and failures."

"Sounds good to me."

"We'll schedule a national broadcast. You can say you launched your own investigation into Maryanne, and regardless of personal embarrassment, you knew you had to divulge the truth," wiping some foam off his mouth.

"She was too weak anyway."

Stayne wrote the speech and Rump delivered it with as much conviction as he could muster. He tried to sound sympathetic for Maryanne, but leveled the blame for the fiasco squarely on her shoulders. His shifting responsibility for creating a national crisis that caused panic and death went over like a lead balloon. And that lead sank his ratings into the mid-teens.

From Max Punch:

"Well, now we find out that Maryanne Curtsy, the one person who tried to humanize Donnie Douchebag, is responsible for the poisoned water hoax. I'm not sure how she could have secretly written all those classified memoranda that assured 10,000 Islamic terrorists had entered America to pollute our precious bodily fluids. AND fob it off as bona fide CIA or FBI or INTERPOL or Junior Space Ranger intelligence. Maybe *she* should be President if she's that clever. Because we need to face the inescapable truth that the vapid, criminal lump of excrescence in the White House really needs to be flushed.

"Which brings me to the derelict House of Representatives. What are you waiting for? Impeachment should have started months ago, and it starts with you. Or are you waiting for your powers to be nullified by Donnie-boy? You don't think he'd hesitate to round you up, do you? I have sources that confirm he was trying to hack into congressional computers and plant treasonous worms insinuating you were planning a coup to de-throne the infant king. Wake up and save our Country!"

THE "ACCIDENT"

Republicans were feeling the heat. Seventy percent of the Country thought Rump should be impeached. Even ardent supporters were aggravated that he couldn't keep any of his campaign promises. Not a single foot of border wall was built, let alone the 10,000 miles needed to surround the Country. No new factories or roads were built. No closed coal mines were re-opened. And most irritatingly, only six people got a free night at a Rump hotel so far, and they were friends of his family.

Rallies were held in Washington and across the Country every weekend with placards insisting "DUMP THE RUMP," "KICK HIS RUMP," "RUMP GRATES ON AMERICA," "RUMP REEKS," and even less decorous insults. Max Punch's editorial was reprinted and sent by activists to every member of Congress several times. Tragically, Punch died suddenly when his car plunged over a bridge near his home. Apparently, something locked the steering wheel and prevented the brakes from working at the same time. Normally a driver would notice a problem well before the mechanics would fail so completely, and in tandem, but hey, things happen. There were rumors about foul play, but the official cause of death was "accidental vehicular mishap."

A NEW EDITORIAL

"Apparently President Rump misunderstood his oath of office just fourteen months ago. He thought the Chief Justice asked, 'Do you swear to violate, desecrate, and urinate all over The Constitution and the American people?' To which he faithfully answered, 'I do.' Because that's exactly what he's done.

"He blames his predecessor, his former electoral opponent, and unnamed leakers for all his woes. But actually, he's the biggest leaker ever to occupy the White House. He's been taking a leak all over law and decency since Day 1. A recent poll of non-partisan historians was published ranking presidents from best to worst in terms of leadership, effectiveness, and fidelity to their office. And Rump placed dead last. With less than half his term served. He was never fit or qualified to assume the Presidency, and he has proven to be a cancer on the body politic that continues to metastasize.

"And so we pick up the cudgel dropped by our late colleague Max Punch. We demand of Congress, WHAT ARE YOU WAITING FOR? WAKE UP AND SAVE OUR COUNTRY!"

The Vice-President, Richard Farthing, was summoned to the Speaker's office.

"Mr. Speaker."

"Mr. Vice President."

—uncomfortable pause—

"Well...are you ready?" asked the Speaker.

"I gather *you* are. Have you drawn up the articles of impeachment?"

"We're working on it. It'll start with suborning a fraudulent national emergency, conspiring with Russia to affect the election, and probably ordering a journalist's car to fail, causing death."

"Ya think?"

"Jesus Dick. How did we get here?"

"We thought he was a joke. During the primaries he said whatever he wanted, and nobody really clocked him on it. He just steamrolled over everyone. But mostly it was that goddamned TV show."

—another uncomfortable pause—

"So it begins?" asked Farthing.

"Unless he's willing to do a Nixon and resign."

"Fat chance. He's either not that bright, or he's more delusional. So to answer your first question, yes, I'm ready."

"Just one thing, for the good of The Party, don't do a Ford. Don't pardon him right away."

EAST-WEST CONVERSATION

"Mr. President Donald. We are ready to release the incriminating Democrat e-mails, but we've heard nothing about the reversal of sanctions. How is that process going?"

"It's hairy Vladimir, very hairy. I can't move on my own, and my political capital is very thin right now, to be perfectly honest with you."

"Yes, I've been reading about your problems, but I have problems of my own. My people are expressing their dissatisfaction. It's being stoked by that chess playing Kasparov bastard. We can't seem to get to him, and not for lack of trying, believe me."

"I sympathize, trust me."

"I need a win."

"I don't know what I can do. To tell you the truth I don't think your bot system can even help me. They're starting the impeachment process and there are Constitutional protocols I'm told. So it wouldn't make any sense now to plant e-mails that Democrats are planning a coup. They can have one for free."

"I understand. But in that case, I need to implement Plan B."

"And that is?"

"We are going to take back The Ukraine. It always was part of Russia anyway, originally."

"Gee Vladimir, that doesn't sound like a good idea, especially right now."

"My popularity shot up right after we took back Crimea. It's what my people want."

"Yeah, but Ukraine is a sovereign nation, and if you go in militarily, we'll have to take action. It's like Saddam Hussein trying to take back Kuwait; it's bad for business."

"Donald, this really is none of *your* business. This does not impact American security in the least."

"Vladimir, don't tell me what is or isn't my business. There are already investigations that you picked my Cabinet appointments. I cannot seem to be your puppet. THERE IS NO COLLUSION! If you move militarily against Ukraine, we will have to move."

"You really want to go to war with me over this Mr. President?"

"You really want to act like Hitler and take over another nation? And you expect us to sit back and take it?"

"This is not your part of the world, and you will stay out of it."

"Who do you think you're talking to Vlado? You mistake me if you think just because we shared broads and caviar that you can tell me what to do."

"A propos, what if I send video of you and those broads at Svetskaya to OCN network, and it's broadcast all over the world? We taped everything, you know."

"You're threatening to blackmail me, you red fink?"
"There are no more red finks, you stupid Donnie douche. I am the leader of the free and proud Russian people."

"And I am still The President of the United States, and you really don't want to fuck with me."

THE CALCULUS

Poutine assumed Rump was all bluster and bluff, after all he hadn't fulfilled any of his American campaign promises, and so Russian tanks rolled into the Ukraine. There were many transplanted Russians living there, and they welcomed the tanks. But the vast majority identified as ethnic Ukrainians, and they fiercely resisted. Poutine tried to mount a decisive siege of Kiev, but the city held defiant. After many brutal skirmishes, 15,000 died in the first three weeks. Rump airlifted heavy artillery to the Ukrainian Army, in addition to offensive aircraft. He also sent several thousand military advisors to coordinate the Ukrainian defense. Poutine expected an easy victory, but he was sorely disappointed.

He did send the sexually compromising footage of Rump in the brothel to OCN, but his timing was off. He should have sent the blackmail well in advance of the Ukrainian invasion. That way Poutine could have claimed Rump was seeking personal revenge for the embarrassment. But since Poutine violated international law by invading a sovereign nation first, public opinion about Rump's moral turpitude was substantially mitigated.

The impeachment process was proceeding through The House, but the polls were inching up in Rump's favor. His military response to Russia proved he wasn't a puppet. Ironically, Poutine may have done him a favor, and Donald felt empowered.

Of course Donald feeling empowered was not necessarily a good thing.

He knew that Poutine had a lot of potentially damaging leverage over him and not just the Svetskaya shenanigans. His business dealings with Russia prior to becoming President were incriminating. His willingness to put Russian selections into his Cabinet was potentially treasonous. All in all it would be better for him, and the world, if Poutine were gone. He vaguely knew that assassination of foreign leaders was prohibited under some obscure law written by some weaklings in some congress at some point. He'd have to work with a network known as "black ops," recently exposed and investigated by USA Today. He didn't know how to access this whatever-it-was, but certainly someone in his circle of advisers could help. The problem was so many of his advisers had ties to

Russia, he wasn't sure which ones had more allegiance to the Kremlin than to him.

He conferred with Stayne how to proceed. Bad choice. Bannan had longstanding ties with Russia unbeknownst to Rump. How ironic that one of the Russkies, against whom his mentor Roy Kong railed so vigorously, was his closest confidante. Bannan actually shared Poutine's core value very deeply, that the world needed a new fascism to control the creeping democratic chaos. Rump was too squishy on this for Stayne's taste. When Bannan informed the Russian leader about Rump's intentions, Vladimir chuckled bitterly, "So, the little douche wants to show who has the bigger balls?"

Of course *he* was not constrained by any statute preventing him from killing anybody he wanted. He mulled over several possibilities including a compromising termination-by-sex scenario involving the Trollops, two of whom were on Moscow's payroll. Hmm, that would be both humiliating and final, a fitting end for the child President. In fact, that would so comport with the public view of him, it would be easy to hide Russia's fingerprints. He set the wheels in motion.

THE WHEELS GO ROUND

One of Poutine's intermediaries between him and the Trollop-spies was Evgeny Karpovsky, an associate of the regime for years. He earned a decent living, but wasn't party to the munificent graft that the upper echelon staff enjoyed. To supplement his income, Evgeny occasionally provided Alex Clamz with stories for Disinfowarz dissemination. The Russian's English was often faulty, and Alex didn't understand a word of Russian. But what matter. He often embellished facts with fancy to hype its entertainment value. A story rarely survived to broadcast with any truth intact.

(Announcer: ATTENTION, ATTENTION, THIS IS A NATIONAL EMERGENCY ALERT. THIS IS NOT A TEST, REPEAT, THIS IS NOT A TEST. AND NOW ALEX CLAMZ.)

"Folks, we have exclusive information that will

threaten every American, and our way of life, perhaps forever. Now sit down, I don't want anyone to fall while listening. Are you sitting? We have just received verified information that Vladimir Poutine has targeted our President Donald D. Rump for death, perhaps with a nuclear attack. We don't know when or where, but I would suggest those living in Washington, New York, and Palm Beach Florida head to your bomb shelters as soon as possible.

"Now there is no need to panic, but make sure you have at least six months of provisions available and plenty of firepower to defend you and yours. At least 150,000 rounds should cover it. And let us pray that somehow through this adversity we will emerge a stronger and more united Country. And rest assured, we will keep broadcasting as long as we are able."

"Holy shit!" thought Rump, "This must be on the level. Clamz didn't even try to sell his suppositories. Maybe if we hit Moscow first, it'll disable their ability to strike us at all. Fuck, I wish I hadn't appointed all those Poutine suggestions to National Security."

He studied (and I use the term loosely) his options and spoke with Bannan, who immediately ratted to Poutine.

"So, the little douche thinks he can solve his problems with a nuclear first strike. It's time to show him, and the world, that Russia is not regional player but a consequential force."

The Washington-Moscow hotline was installed after the Cuban Missile Crisis in 1962, to prevent nuclear war by miscalculation. More recently it had been used by Rump and Poutine to talk about their mutually unpleasant poll numbers. But those days of camaraderie were long over. Either could have phoned the other to clarify misconceptions, but neither would. From each of their hyper-masculine perspectives, whoever called first would be considered the weaker. And so the world seemed headed toward nuclear annihilation.

WHAT WE WILL MISS AFTER NUCLEAR ANNIHILATION

Love. Love leading to sex. Sex all by itself. Flirting. Marriage. A good meal. A good walk. Movies. Some TV. Internet surfing. Travel. Pets. Trees. Gardens. Friends. A day at the beach. Laughter. Having children. Watching them grow. A good foot massage. A good head massage. Reading. Music. Theatre. Museums. Amusement Parks. Chocolate. Play. Singing. Fun. Farmers Markets. Super suppositories. Yoga. Steam Rooms. Jacuzzis. Sports. Toe wiggling. Conversation. Dissent. Prayer. Holding hands. Smiling. Holidays. Dreaming. Planning for the future. Overcoming obstacles. Watching a sunset. Watching a sunrise. A gentle rain. Rainbows. Great art. Promising art. Wonderful scents. The warmth of the sun. A cool breeze. Swimming. Bicycling. Driving with little traffic. New discoveries. Finding something lost. Learning a new

skill. Waking from a nightmare. A new President. Breathing. Dying a natural death. Our lives.
(Add your own here.)

WHAT WILL NOT BE MISSED

Social media and reality television.

BUT...

Each leader realized there was a value in striking first, but they had to make sure their personal bunkers were well stocked. Nobody thought they'd ever be used, so emergency provisions were not refreshed on a regular basis. In fact, some sell-by dates were stamped in the last millennium. And these men had expensive tastes. No canned sardines and freeze-dried ice cream for them. Dry roasted nuts and protein bars for six months or longer? You must be kidding. They each had personal assistants comb the gourmet stores for the most delicious comestibles that had some kind of shelf life. The purpose of the delicacy hunt was never divulged, so the shoppers could only imagine it was for some kind of big blowout. Ahem.

Rump was torn about the Trollops. He knew they weren't family members, and therefore couldn't join him in the bunker. But he had feelings for them. He wanted to give them each a tumble before...the next phase. He made appointments with them individually, and then all together for one last "group hug."

Poutine fell into a bit of a morose Slavic depression. He would miss much of this world. And he would miss being Valya: Empress of All the Russias. Valya hadn't performed in a long time and the Russian strongman knew he couldn't bring the costume, heels, false eyelashes, lipstick and feathered boa into the bunker. Vladimir decided to give one last performance for a close circle of friends in his private apartment.

Rump greeted each girl in his patent leather jockstrap, the picture of potent, virile leadership. Except maybe not so potent. It usually took him ten minutes or so to finish (foreplay was not his strong suit), so he booked the girls every fifteen minutes. But he seemed to be mentally pre-occupied with something or other, because he suffered a rare bout of erectile dysfunction. He never needed Viagra, so none was available. The girls therefore needed extra time to try to complete their useful function competently and so were stacked up in the room outside his chamber like flights waiting to land.

Evgeny was at the microphone in the lounge area of the Presidential apartment, addressing the expectant audience.

"And now, for her farewell appearance, hands together for Valya: Empress of All The Russias."

And Valya slinked into the spotlight, silver lamé sparkling, makeup done to perfection, the feathered boa wrapped around her body like a jealous lover. Much applause and whistles of appreciation. She manipulated that boa like a seasoned seductress, swirling it gently around the heads of her all-male audience, and flinging part of it sideways to expose her beautifully enhanced prosthetic bosom. That boa gave her a sensual freedom unknown to the Russian Head of State. Finally she launched into song.

"Falling in love again, never wanted to..."

The fourth girl, Kylie, emerged from Rump's chamber dripping with sweat.

"Jeez it's hard work to get him hard. You've got to really relax your mouth and neck 'til he gets it kind of up and then it deflates. So Trixie, do your best."

Trixie was confident. She was a top fellatrix and knew lots of little tricks. She entered the chamber and found Donald on the bed breathing heavily and very red in the face. Even his hair looked tense and frustrated.

"Mr. President do you want to take a break?"

"NO! I've been waiting for you Trixie. You know you're the best. So come here and suck that golf ball through the garden hose."

She assumed the position and went to work. She tried slow, fast, fluted tongue-work, deep throat, rimming, and prostate stimulation. Gradually there was a flicker of life.

"Straddle me."

She did as commanded, and a semi-erection was formed.

"In."

She pocketed the shaft and moaned encouragingly. He thrust up and down with some effort, but after a couple minutes, deflated.

"...*Men cluster to me like moths around a flame, and if their wings burn, I know I'm not to blame. Falling in love again, never wanted to, what am I to do, I just can't help it.*" She sashayed around the room kissing men on the top of their heads, boa trailing behind. It was actually quite touching, Vladimir saying goodbye to some of his friends in light of what was to come. As he moved around, the trailing boa started to hamper his mobility somewhat. Unbeknownst to him it had wrapped around one of the spotlight poles.

"Squeeze me inside!"

She applied her pelvic muscles to little effect.

"Dammit!"

"Shh, honey, just relax a little." She bent down and put her hands around his neck. They had played with erotic asphyxia a couple times, and it always did the trick. She squeezed just a little. He gasped appreciatively,

"More."

She complied and could feel him rise within her.

"Yes."

It was working, and he was getting close. Frankly so was she. She had never been quite so turned on. She squeezed harder.

"Oh God," as he thrust rapidly up and down. But his face was turning from red to bluish. She bounced up and down faster, and squeezed his throat harder. They were both about to explode.

Poutine was annoyed that his moves were being constrained by the boa. Of course Valya would have taken it in stride and worked her way around the problem. But Vladimir was not about to have his final performance humiliated by a mechanical problem. So he gave a strong sharp tug, bringing the spotlight crashing down upon his head, killing him instantly.

Trixie was about to have the orgasm of her life. As it turns out, so was Donald. As she climaxed and squeezed his throat very hard, Rump came and went. It may seem unfair, but for many he received "the consummation devoutly to be wished." And to his credit he stayed rock hard throughout, although that was actually creeping *rigor mortis.*

BY THE SKIN OF OUR TEETH

Richard Farthing took the Oath of Office at almost the exact time that Viktor Davidoff, Poutine's second, ascended to the Presidency of Russia. Immediately thereafter, they spoke on The Hotline and gave each other assurance that neither of them was planning a nuclear, or any type of attack in the foreseeable future. They also agreed on United Nations arbitration for the Ukrainian incursion.

The world would not know how close it came to an extinction-level event until much later. Historians would mull over l'affair de Rump for years to come. If not for the false friendship between him and Poutine that led to catastrophic miscalculation, would the impeachment process have run its course and expelled Donald? Probably. If the political parties had insisted on complete and verified financial transparency and refused to allow conflicts of interest regardless of legal technicalities, would Rump have been disqualified from nomination? Possibly.

If not for Paycheck, would Rump have had the platform or popularity to run for President in the first place? Who knows?

So was Donald D. Rump a uniquely toxic anomaly? Can Democrats and Republicans nominate Presidential candidates with intelligence, integrity and charisma? Do enough Americans care about the first two qualities anymore to make a difference? Can a critical mass of Americans insist on facts being the basis of what's true, and discard patent bullshit? Do Hitler's unfortunate maxims still pertain?

Stay tuned.

"Trumpty-Dumpty wanted a wall
Trumpty-Dumpty had a great fall
All the law's women and all the law's men
Tried to put us together again."

— Heard on the Playground

THANK YOU

Thank you for reading *The Haircut Who Would Be King*. If you enjoyed it, please take time to leave a review on Amazon, Barnes and Noble, Goodreads, or one of your other favorite online retailers.

Reviews are the best way to show your support for an author and to help new readers discover their books.

CPSIA information can be obtained
at www.ICGtesting.com
Printed in the USA
LVHW081108030420
652122LV00022B/3210